# #Justice

## (Hashtag Justice)

By

Mike Leon

# This Strong Woman Thought She Would Be Murdered. You Won't Believe What Happens Next.

## It's Literally The Most Chilling Thing.

"You really should stay away from the windows, Ms. Saito." The coldly professional suggestion comes from the stockier of the two well-dressed men in Izumi's living room. She lets go of the thick vinyl vertical blind between her fingers and it swings back into place with the others.

"Do you think they could be watching?" Izumi asks, her tone falling somewhere between worry and disgust. "Through the windows?"

"I doubt it," the bodyguard replies. He is bald and black skinned, with a roguishly handsome scar on his left temple—a real mandingo, and one that would piss off her traditional Japanese parents for an added bonus. She wishes she could remember his name. She'll have to look at his business card again later. "It's just a standard precaution."

"Right." Izumi moves away from the floor-to-ceiling window and sits down on the white sectional that occupies most of the room. On the opposite end of the couch, the other bodyguard sits with his legs crossed, scrolling through some social networking site or another on his cell phone. He's older, flabbier, white, and eerily quiet. His presence makes Izumi more nervous than she was already. She reaches for the TV remote and turns on the big flat panel television across the room just to have some kind of noise to cover the awkward silence. "So do you do this kind of thing a lot?" Izumi asks, directing her attention at the friendlier, better looking man.

"Exactly like this? We're usually out in public more, concert details for pop stars, politicians. But we do our share of stakeouts. Me and Bill have seen just about everything. Isn't that right, Bill?"

Bill nods without looking away from his cell phone. "Yup," he confirms.

"Shouldn't you be more . . . alert?" Izumi frowns at him, and he barely registers her concern.

"Nothing is gonna happen in here," Bill says. His tone is a little more gruff than Izumi can appreciate.

"What my partner means is it's the streets you have to worry about," his hunky colleague says. "Out there, danger can come at you from any direction any time. Some psycho might pull a gun, a knife, weirder stuff, for no reason at all. Just last month I stopped a guy from injecting Brittany Perkins with a syringe full of his own blood. He said she was a demon or something. But this is a different story. We're ten floors up. The only way in or out is that restricted elevator. Even if somebody got a key for it then they have to go through me and Bill as soon as they come through the door."

"I'd put thirteen in 'em without asking any questions," Bill grumbles lazily.

"And he will," the handsome guard says. "Bill was a contractor in Afghanistan. He's seen his share."

"What if they find another way?" Izumi asks.

"There's no other way. Not unless your creepy stalker can order a drone strike."

"Does that happen often?"

"No. That never happens. It's just a joke."

"Oh. Okay."

Izumi turns her attention to the TV and flips through Netflix for a bit before finally settling on an old episode of *Smallville*, a show she watched when she was a kid. The familiarity of it is somehow comforting now. Midway through the opening credits, she gets a call that she wants to ignore, but decides to take anyway, just to keep up appearances.

"Hey, bitch," Izumi says, answering the phone with her usual playful invective.

"Hi," Leslie responds with slightly drawn out uncertainty. The junior editor never seems to know quite how to deal with Izumi's wholly empowered attitude. "You okay?"

"Hells yeah. Why wouldn't I be?"

"It's just, I heard you hired bodyguards?"

"What? That's crazy. Why would I do that?" Izumi shifts her eyes instinctively to the bodyguards in her living room.

"Because of what happened to all those freelance writers. I don't know. It's just what I heard."

"None of that stuff is true. Those were accidents. It's just a spooky coincidence."

"I hope so. Some of us can't afford hired gunslingers."

"Girl, you know I got your back. If anything happens, I'll get you the A-Team, and the other staff too. But nothing happened. Nobody is out to get us. That's crazy talk."

"You're probably right."

"You know I am. Now tell me that dolphin poaching story is live."

"Yeah. It turned out it wasn't a dolphin, it was a thresher shark."

"Ew."

"Yeah. I used a stock photo of a bottlenose dolphin and we can publish an update later if someone complains."

"That's my girl. Awesome."

"George from Slacktivision called. He wants Gamestiq to give *Call of Honor: Incalculable Warfare 2* at least a nine out of ten score."

"How desperate did he sound?"

"Desperate enough to buy us all Caribbean cruises again."

"Awesome. I could use some sun."

"There's a video charting on YouTube. Two pre-op transsexuals can't get dates with straight men."

"They have dicks?"

"Yeah."

"We can still swing that. Headline: These Ladies Show Bigotry is Still Alive and Well."

"Tomorrow's listicles are Five Things Only Sociopaths Watch on TV, Fifteen Celebrities Who Just Can't Even, and Eight Times We Fell in Love with Pie."

"Didn't we do that one already?"

"No. We did Eleven Times We Fell in Love with Pie."

"Okay good. Run it."

"Is everything okay?"

"What would be wrong?"

"You just seem a little off tonight."

"I can't remember every listicle we ever post . . ." *Smallville* suddenly turns to a tidal wave of crunched colors and the home theater speaker bar mounted on the wall below the TV emits an oscillating womp womp. The lights fizzle and the living room darkens. Izumi squeals with fright, and Bill pulls a gun from the holster under his arm, but everything in the room is back to normal as quickly as it began.

"Izumi?" Leslie calls out from the phone now lowered away from Izumi's ear.

"What was that?" Bill says. "A power surge? That happen a lot in here?"

"No." Izumi shakes her head, glancing back at the familiar face of Tom Welling now back in focus on the TV screen.

"Maybe the people downstairs decided to run all the appliances at the same time. Who knows . . ."

"But that's never happened before . . ."

"Well it doesn't make any difference," the handsome one says, grinning back at her from his place in front of the elevator doors. "The—" he stops suddenly, his smirk shifting to an expression of astonishment at something beyond Izumi, behind her. "What the?" He goes for his gun.

Izumi turns and sees something more outlandish than she could ever have imagined.

"Drop it!" Bill shouts. "Drop the knife!" Izumi didn't even see the weapon. She was too focused on the empty black eyes of the evil figure in her living room. "Drop it! Drop it!"

Then the shots ring out like needles in her ears. *Bam! Bam! Bam!* Izumi dives from the sofa, covering her head and closing her eyes. She makes it to the corner near the elevator to cower behind her gunmen in the brief lull between the shots in which Bill says "What the hell?" Then the men are shooting more. Then something warm and wet sprays across her face. Izumi wipes it away and opens her eyes to the sight of deep red muck smeared on her fingers. The penthouse is silent.

# #JUSTICE

Izumi turns up and screams at the horrifying figure leaning over her body. She screams at the dead men with their empty guns. She screams as she goes through the huge window and the glass shards cut into her flesh. She screams all the way to the pavement ten stories below.

# INT. THE BLACK OMEN - NIGHT

The thumping beat and synthesized industrial clatter of a musician called Perturbator rattles through Sid's head as he lies back against the black leather of the sectional sofa that spans the rear wall of the VIP room at the Black Omen. Pink fog refracts the UV light from the purple bulbs overhead. Ahead of him, Lily Hoffman allows a microns-thick slip of fabric she calls a dress to fall to the floor and reveal her luscious naked figure.

Lily is a small woman, short and pale like copy paper. Her skin glows a bright shade of violet under the lights, and her many gothic black tattoos are voids in the purple haze. She runs her black fingernails through her raven hair as she turns for him. Some women are described as top heavy. Lily is the reverse. Her narrow shoulders and itty-bitty waist give way to battle-axe hips and a big bubble butt that draws Sid's eyes in a pendulum motion as she drops her black g-string panties down around the 7-inch platform stiletto stilts she calls shoes. A colored back light silhouettes the gap between her thighs and causes Sid's pulse to pound with furious anticipation.

She turns and stilt-walks toward him, stepping up to a riser with a golden pole at the foot of the couch. She leans over him, hanging one-armed from the pole, her lengthy hair swinging above his lap like a bobbing string to tease a cat.

"I knew you couldn't stay away from me for long," Lily says, licking her deathly black lips.

"I was just in town on business," Sid says. "Don't let it go to your head."

"No?" Lily chirps. "Don't you want *it* to go to my head?" She steps down from the riser, planting her dagger heels on the sofa cushion on either side of him. She swipes her middle finger through her waxy smooth labia only inches from his nose, trailing wetness up to the Wasteland tattoo that rides her pubic bone. "Or would you rather put it somewhere else?"

Sid doesn't know what to say to that. He doesn't want to say anything. He just wants to be inside her. He plants his hands on her butt and draws her in. She moans as he slips his tongue into her salty wetness and closes his eyes.

"Mmmm. Deeper," she whispers. Sid presses into her even harder and she squeaks reflexively. "Deeper," she still insists.

He hugs her thighs, pulling her in with his considerable strength and tearing at her flesh like a hungry wolf.

"Harder. Deeper!" she exclaims.

Sid pulls away and glares doubtfully up into Lily's gleaming blue eyes. She smiles back at him.

"Like this," she says, reaching down to spread herself open with both hands. Her vagina stretches to the absolute physical limit, until he can see all the way to the fleshy pink end of it, then beyond. Her inner lips open wider than his head and sprout dozens of crocodile fangs that snap shut around Sid's neck.

He roars and punches at Lily's soft flesh, battering her legs and belly with a rain of blows that would shatter men's bones.

"Don't fight it," Lily squeals, throwing her head back and howling with pleasure. "I want you inside me forever . . . and ever . . . and ever . . ." Sid feels her lips sliding past his shoulders as she swallows him in. Her cervix slurps loudly as he passes through it into the swampy darkness beyond. Her womb seals around him like a pool cover drowning a child who has fallen in.

Sid's eyes snap open and he is awake in the neon glow of his bedroom. His sweaty skin is illuminated through his closed blinds by the giant Jesus Saves sign directly across the street.

He turns and observes the gentle breathing of the woman in his bed. Sapphire. That's what she calls herself anyway. She's blond and wispy. Tall and busty. Her face is gaunt with age she won't be able to lie about much longer. She says she's twenty-five and working on her thesis at the university a few miles away, that she likes to party, always with an emphasis on party meant to convey something Sid does not understand. This is her story anyway. In truth, she is thirty-eight, divorced twice, and spends her days sharing custody of three children who are almost Sid's age. She is not in school, and appears to generate income solely from sex work. Her real name is Jennifer. He learned all of this by surveilling her for two weeks, though that was hardly necessary. Her cover was paper thin. He can't understand how a call girl, who does exactly what call girls do, procured from a call girl service no less, could then claim she is not a call girl and think no one would poke holes in that story.

# #JUSTICE

Normally Sid leers at pretty women the way he looks at juicy steak, but after that nightmare he can't help looking at Sapphire like the meat's gone bad. He slips from the bed as a silent shadow, leaving the call girl undisturbed. He picks up his discarded shorts and heads out into the hall, closing the door behind him. He could watch some TV in the den downstairs. TV is stupid, but not completely without merit, and he's been watching a lot of it lately in an effort to catch up with the seemingly constant stream of pithy little quotes and references people make around him. A few days ago someone said "No soup for you!" in a mimicked Arabian accent, and Sid knew what that was. Still, he tends toward the grittier visual entertainment. *Robocop* and *The Road Warrior* were among some recent viewings, but the best one so far was a movie called *Demolition Man*, which Sid found particularly relatable.

The firehouse in which he currently resides is a three floor brick building, but as tall as some five floor buildings when accounting for the high ceilings. It dates back to the early 1900s, and hasn't been used by actual firefighters for two decades. Player procured it for them at auction. Sid heads down the hallway from his room on the third floor toward the steel fire pole near the rear of the building, which he snatches and glides down toward the bottom floor, a wide open garage with space enough for two fire trucks-or a black utility van loaded with more munitions, a bunch more munitions locked in a steel cage, a computer terminal, and a rug with a sofa and television.

Sid silently lowers through the hole in the ceiling and spots Mary Sue's bright pink hair at the far end of the garage, her attention swiveling back and forth between computer LCD displays on the desk in front of her. Sid clamps his hands on the pole and halts his slide. She hasn't noticed him yet, which is good. Something about her excessive femininity seems especially off-putting after that creepy dream. In fact, just dealing with Mary Sue in general is a little off-putting all the time.

Mary Sue Jadefire Sakura Ravencaller is a strange enigma. The plucky little girl is a lot of things, both descriptively and vocationally. Despite only being sixteen years old, she has a plethora of advanced degrees, is a doctor, is an Olympic gold medalist, hacks computers like a pro, and has a body hotter than the sun. Where did she come from? Sid has not even the slightest idea. He only knows she doesn't put out, and that's enough to keep his interest limited.

Sid climbs back up the pole to the third floor and hops off, trying to decide what else he could do to clear his head. That's when he notices the bright orange electrical extension cord which is dangling down the red ladder leading up to the open roof access hatch at the top of the steps. He traces it to an outlet in the corner, then back up the ladder. He raises an eyebrow to the peculiarity, then begins climbing.

On top of the building Sid finds Bruce Freeman sitting on a collapsible nylon chair, bathed in the blood red glow of the sign across the way. The other end of the extension cord lies at his feet with a portable radio and another cable running to something in Bruce's hands. Bruce leans over the arm of the chair and plucks up a longneck bottle of beer from a cardboard six-pack carton on the other side of the chair and pops the cap with a little bottle opener. The radio crackles with a fuzzy conversation.

Well, Bart, they didn't probe me or nothing like that. But they did take me to the rings of Saturn where their secret base is. See, it's invisible to our telescopes. And they had a message for me. They said they've been watching us for a long time and Jesus, he was one of them in disguise, and we shoulda listened to him when he tried to warn us, because this problem with the wheat gluten is because of that.

Wheat gluten?

That's right. Wheat gluten is the first seal, Bart. Of the apocalypse. Think about it. You ever hear of a gluten intolerance 200 years ago?

"What are you doing up here?" Sid says, startling Bruce.

"Yeh," Bruce chokes as he whips his head around to make eye contact. "Shit. Make noise or something will ya? God damn. Gonna get a bell to hang on you like a cat." Bruce is a former CIA agent, former contract commando for Graveyard, and the former manager of the GameStop where Sid used to work. They met when Sid single handedly annihilated Graveyard's headquarters last year to finally stop them from sending kill teams, commandos, and assassins to kill him everywhere he went. Bruce was the only operator Sid encountered in the building who didn't try to fight him, opting to throw down his gun and give up instead. They've had several adventures together since.

"What are you doing on the roof?" Sid says.

"*Chrono Trigger*, booze, and *Conspiratalk*." Walking around the chair, Sid can see that the object of Bruce's attention is a handheld video game system. "It's on all night. This guy Bart Gong takes calls from people that've seen Bigfoot and been abducted by aliens and shit like that."

In 1986 while I was a janitor at IBM I had a sexual encounter with an artificial intelligence-an android to be exact.

"Sometimes they talk about regular shit like serial killers or end-of-the-world asteroid collisions or some shit." Bruce continues, smirking as though he knows some secret to it all. "But it's a lot more entertaining if you got insider info, cause you know for sure which callers are actually on to something and which callers are just crazy. Here's a hint. None of them are onto something."

They need white male sperm and Chinese ovum to mix with their circuits so they can make a race of half human, half Chinese, half robot hybrids that can survive in a vacuum.

"You think anyone will notice if I shoot the Jesus sign out?"

"Yeah. I wouldn't fuck with it. We don't need the cops snooping around here. We got more NFA guns than John Woo up in this bitch and not a registration for one of them."

Sid grunts. "I hate that thing."

"The NFA?"

"The sign. It's like living under a heat lamp."

"Don't cry to me. I told you to stay in the basement."

"It's not as defensible."

Because the sasquatch peoples have a treaty with the vampires which they recently renewed, Bart. They're working together now because they're afraid of the return of the icons, which could destroy them both.

"That guy sounds like an idiot." Sid laughs. "There's no such thing as vampires."

"Didn't you kill a werewolf once?"

"Yeah. What about it?"

"Nothing. What are you doing up here anyway? I thought you were banging whatshertits? Amber?"

"Sapphire."

"Right. Sapphire. How come chicks are always Amber or Sapphire? What about all the other gemstones? How come you never meet a chick named Peridot or Tanzanite?"

Sid shrugs. "We fucked for three hours, but she got tired so I let her sleep. Then I had that weird dream again."

"Shit. You gotta get this chick off your brain."

"She's not on my brain," Sid growls back.

"Recurring nightmare where she swallows you with her pussy like a snake? That's as on the brain as it gets, man. That's some fucked up Freud shit there. It's symbolic. See the pussy is this thing you gotta keep coming back to. She lures you in with it, and then . . .SNAP! It's like a trap you can't get out of. You're stuck in that shit forever. Cause that's what the pussy really is. Except I mean usually a bitch put a baby on you or get some alimony or some normal shit like that. This Lily chick is crazier than all that, *and* she got the ESP, so you're double fucked."

"Extra sensory perception?"

"Elusive snapping pussy. That's the pussy you can't never leave behind."

"I'm gonna leave it behind."

"You can't. I'm telling you. No way. I know this shit. Her name was Jada Harris. Bitch set my car on fire and I still went back to her."

"What if I find a girl with an even better ESP?"

"You never will. That's the whole thing about the ESP. You never find another one that's as good as that one."

"That's stupid, Bruce. There are billions of women in the world. The chances that I already found the best piece of ass out of all of them, on my first try-it's impossible."

"You're missing what I'm saying. It's not about the best. It's about them being up here." Bruce taps the side of his head. "It's all in here is the problem. You can never let it go."

I think we have time for one more caller. We're on the line with Jamie. You're on the air.

The idea Bruce presents is disconcerting, but not entirely unsupported by the evidence. Since the Red Scare incident, Sid has been with numerous women in a sexual capacity. Most them were prostitutes. All of them were beautiful. All of them fell short, if only slightly, of the bar set by Lily Hoffman.

Bart? I don't have much time. I know they're triangulating my position. I'm in a lot of trouble. I'm being hunted by Kill Team One.

"Hey they're talking about you," Bruce chuckles.

"Do they talk about me a lot?" Sid questions, slightly amused by this turn.

"Oh yeah. Conspiracy people have all kinds of theories about the NWO. Some of the stories from special ops guys who worked with your dad have kinda trickled down to these people. Most of them think you're some kind of alien and you did 9/11, and those are actually the more realistic sounding theories. Bart did a whole show about it last year."

I've been running for two days. I haven't slept. Wherever I go, he finds me. I can tell when he's watching. He's, oh God, he's horrible. His eyes are so black. They're like animal eyes. There's nothing in them.

"Maybe this clown really has met you before," Bruce remarks in jest. Clearly Sid is not trying to kill this radio caller. Sid has been busy for a few months, mostly recovering from a broken jaw and banging lots of whores.

I need to make public what I know-I know your audience will listen. These people can't get away with this. There are names. Scottie Fitch, Jaqclyn Davis, Karen Masters . . .

Should you be saying these full names on the air?

Yes, Bart! They killed them! They killed them all! Jennifer Marquits, Lydia James, Christina Jawadi, Brian Kemp, and now Izumi Saito. All those people were murdered by Kill Team One in the last six weeks! The police won't do anything! They're a part of it! We're talking about the deep state here!

Do you have any idea what they want, Jamie? Do you know something the government doesn't want out there?

No! I don't know what they want! I don't know what I did! I don't have any state secrets! I'm not a spy! I'm not a researcher at Area 51! I'm a specialist in postmodern literature! Kinkos wouldn't even hire me!

Suddenly, Sid experiences a jolt of awareness that ends whatever minimal entertainment he derived from the radio program. He cringes as he stares out into the dark, focusing on the rising and falling red blinkers of a distant radio tower. When he last spoke to Helen Anderson at Graveyard, she had used that same word: postmodern. She had used it with ominous undertones, and claimed the fate of the world was at stake. Sid ignored her for several reasons, the foremost being that Graveyard almost constantly, and dubiously, claims the fate of the world is at stake. It's usually just a ploy to get people to serve their agenda.

Oh God! What is—They're—He's here! Die! Die, pig!

The broadcast cuts out. Sid and Bruce glance curiously to each other as they wait through seven seconds of just the faint whiny breathing of silent AM transmission.

"What the hell was that?" Sid says.

"It sounds like you got him." Bruce wavers on other possibilities. "I dunno, man. This show gets a lot of crank calls. One time some guy called pretending to be Chris Redfield from *Resident Evil*. He had this whole bit prepared about the Umbrella Corporation."

Okay, we're sorry about that, folks. I had to cut out the last part of that call. Very strange. How much of that did you all hear? I'm not sure what got out. We'll go to our wild card line with Bill. Bill, you're on the line.

"It was probably a prank," Bruce uneasily declares, as though he's trying to convince himself more than anyone else.

Sid is not so set on the explanation. "He said something about postmodernism."

"Like the future?"

"No," Sid grunts. "It's some kind of thing from *Buffy the Vampire Slayer*. Graveyard thinks it has something to do with the end of the world."

"Hold up." The tone of Bruce's voice rises with intrigue. "You think that call was real?"

"No." Sid's dismissal is too quick and forced to be authentic. He knows as soon as he says the words. He has never been a good liar. I think we should just forget this whole thing."

"What? Graveyard, or maybe just some random guy, is out there murdering innocent people and letting everybody think it's you and you're just gonna let that go?"

"Sure. Why not?"

"Your rep, homie. Your rep."

"You just said they think I did 9/11." Sid briefly compares these imaginings about him to the genuine article, and finds them not too terribly dissimilar. "And I kill people all the time. Whatever they're saying about me is a drop in the bucket."

"What about the end of the world though? What if it's true?"

Sid waves off the suggestion dismissively. "It never is. You really want to get wrapped up in some Graveyard problem and end up fighting the lizard king or a shadow monster or Cabal neo-soldiers or something like that?" Sid's efforts over the last few months with the Player have been exceedingly smooth and transparent compared to any of the work he ever did involving Graveyard. It turned out that his initial distrust of the mysterious computer voice was largely baseless. The Player has only asked Sid to conduct some very simple operations, including the assassination of an active child murdering pedophile in Montana, the annihilation of a small ISIS splinter group in Florida, and the destruction of a Christian fundamentalist cult's sarin gas stockpile. Sid thinks all of those activities were an objectively worthwhile use of his time and capabilities. Also, he got whore money.

"That is a good point actually."

"See what I mean? With the Player it's all easy mode. All I have to do is lay a smackdown on regular terrorists once in a while and I get money for whores and you get money for . . . whatever you people do with money—other stuff besides whores."

"I still don't get how you can't wrap your head around money."

"I understand it. I just don't need it, except for whores."

"What about food?"

"I kill it or steal it."

"Clothes?"

"Steal them."

"Cars? Guns?"

"Also steal them."

"But you can't steal whores."

"You *can*. It's just nasty."

"You never try good old fashioned charm?"

Sid doesn't dignify that question with a spoken response. He only frowns back at Bruce to signal that he thinks the suggestion is stupid. Women are ambiguous and fickle creatures. Attempting to woo them without cash has proven extremely inefficient, and produced wildly variable results.

"Alright. So this thing with the mysterious phone call to Bart Gong didn't happen."

"Didn't happen. We don't know anything about it."

"Absolutely nothing."

"You guys!" Mary Sue says, excitedly climbing through the roof access hatch to join them in the red glow of the city rooftop. "You'll never believe this! Somebody just called in to Conspiratalk about you!"

"Fuck," Sid snarls.

# INT. FIREHOUSE - DAWN

Sid wonders if there is still a way to sabotage this clusterfuck of an operation before it gets off the ground. He sits on one of the swivel chairs near the equipment cage at the rear of the garage, his feet planted in a wide stance and his hands behind his head, holding it up as he grimaces at the florescent lights lining the ceiling.

"It was probably just a made up story," he insists.

"I don't think so," Mary Sue sheepishly denies. She's always sheepish, even when she's shutting him down. Sid doesn't like that about her. He has no patience for mealy mouthed pleasantries. "I checked the names the caller listed against a database of violent crimes committed in the last month and I got hits for all of them."

"You can do that?"

"Sure," Mary Sue giggles. She sounds like she's six. "I hack the FBI and police all the time as a white hat consultant."

"Tell him about the pattern." The second voice comes from the conference phone on the desk next to Mary Sue's mousepad. It belongs to the Player, the mysterious benefactor who directs and bankrolls Sid's operations. He doesn't know who the Player is, though he has some theories, and the entity only speaks to him via electronic devices, always with a disguised voice. For the last week, Player has been emulating Holly the supercomputer from a British television show called

Red Dwarf. Sid tried to watch one episode of the show, but thought it was stupid and turned it off.

"What pattern?" Bruce says. Sid's admonishing eyes dart over to the spy hunter, but it's far too late to stop this conversation from going where it's going to go.

"All of the victims were killed under eerily similar circumstances," Mary says. "I mean, if you know what to look for. Otherwise they just look like accidents, and that was the conclusion of most of the investigations."

"So somebody is bumping these people off and making it look accidental." Sid shrugs. "It happens."

"Well. . . It's just that they didn't make an effort to cover their tracks. I don't know. I'm just a stupid girl."

Player jumps in where Mary Sue has faltered. "What she's saying is the murders appearing accidental is incidental," Player says.

"You mean that they appear accidental is accidental?" Sid says.

"No. Incidental. As in they appear that way by an unintentional consequence of being done."

"Huh?"

"Jennifer Marquits was found in her locked apartment. No sign of forced entry and the chain bolts on the door were all still fastened."

"So the killer came in an open window. Left the same way."

"On the twenty-second floor?"

Sid shrugs. "I would."

"You're sort of exceptional," Mary Sue says.

"You hear that?" Sid smirks smugly at Bruce. "I'm exceptional." Bruce snickers and wags his head, but they only receive a blank stare from Mary Sue.

"I don't get it," she says.

"Let's stay on topic here," the Player interrupts. "Scottie Fitch jumped through a plate glass window from his apartment. The police ruled it a suicide even though the apartment was a wreck like there had been a fight. Again, no signs of forced entry and the doors were bolted from the inside."

"It's another window," Sid reasons. "Every time somebody falls out of a window that's suddenly my problem?"

"Not all of them were windows. Christina Jawadi fell onto the tracks in front of a New York subway train. Jaqclyn Davis drove off a highway overpass. Karen Masters apparently hung herself from a drain pipe in her office's parking garage-after getting a promotion at work and a marriage proposal from her multimillionaire venture capitalist boyfriend in the preceding twenty-four hours." Player halts for a few seconds as though waiting for Sid to pick up some unspoken conclusion. "She said yes."

"So this guy looked up a bunch of random accidents and suicides and made up a story. I still don't see how any of this is related."

The Player is not impeded. "Every one of the victims was an internet journalist."

"Who isn't?" Bruce snorts.

"This is serious. Davis wrote for *Trigger*. Jawadi was the culture editor for *ProgVoice*. Karen Masters wrote a number of think pieces for *Futura* under a pseudonym."

"That one took some time to connect," Mary says.

"Every one of these people wrote at least one article for a major site. The list is like a who's who of fake news: *UpFeed*, *The Rag*, *The Duffington Pole*, *Data Battles*, *Rubbernecker*, the *Daily Beast*, *Pixelmap*. . ."

Bruce seems taken aback by the last mention. "The video game site with the guy who broke down crying during the *Call of Honor* review?"

"That's the one."

"He cried about a video game?" Sid laughs.

"Motherfucker got all weepy cause the guns looked too real. How you gonna review first person shooters if you're afraid of guns?"

"The most recent victim wasn't nearly so afraid of guns," Player says. "Izumi Saito had two armed guards in her apartment at the time of the murder. Real mercenaries. They fired twenty seven rounds before someone stabbed them to death with a kitchen knife. Then the killer threw Saito through a window."

"What's with all the windows and trains and shit?" Bruce says. "Wouldn't it be easier to cap a bitch?"

"To make them look like accidents?" Mary Sue suggests. "Cover up the murders?"

"Nah." Bruce waves off the idea. "When you just did a slice and dice on the body guards ten feet away? That doesn't cover shit."

"What if the killer can't carry weapons with him? Assuming the kitchen knife came from Saito's kitchen, all of the murders were committed with objects found at the scene or no weapons at all."

"All of them were push-into-traffic kinda things." Bruce nods. "Except the stabby one. It's kinda weird."

"We need to find the person who made that call. Jamie. He seems to know more about this."

"We could go to the radio station—get their call logs. Run them through a crisscross directory and find the pay phone."

"A crisscross directory?" Mary Sue shakes her head. A crisscross directory is a telephone book organized in order by number rather than name, which can then be used to track phone calls back to their point of origin. The term has become archaic with the advent of computer directories that can be searched by any piece of relevant information, cell phones that can place calls from anywhere, and the ensuing decline of printed hardcopy phone books.

"Something us old people used to use." Bruce is much older than Sid or Mary Sue, though Sid does not know exactly how old. Sid only knows about crisscross directories because of his old man's stubborn skiptracing lessons.

"Aw, come on!" Sid grumbles. "You're on board with this now too?"

Bruce winces, clearly having some discomfort related to this admission. "It's just it's really interesting. And there's the whole postmodern thing."

"The postmodern thing?"

"Fuck," Sid growls. Now that cat is out of the bag.

"Graveyard has some kinda interest in postmodernism," Bruce explains. "Whatever that is."

"What?!" the synthesized voice clips. "How do you know?"

Sid groans and rolls his eyes. "Helen Anderson asked me a bunch of questions about it the last time I saw her."

"Why didn't you say something?"

"I've told you this before. I don't want to get involved with those assholes again. When you get wrapped up with Graveyard, shit gets weird fast. You think you're just doing some normal wetworks, then suddenly you're in a flying sex dungeon fighting bengal tigers with a combat knife while a warlock shoots force lightning at you from a crystal skull."

"Sid," Bruce leans in to speak some truth. "I'm currently having a conversation with a mysterious robot voice, a guy who is impervious to bullets for absolutely no reason anyone can explain, and a pink haired sixteen-year-old rocket scientist neurosurgeon who just hacked the FBI from an iMac. From where I stand, shit got weird a while ago."

"Okay, then you guys go tackle this thing then. I'll be here with the hookers and the Netflix app. Knock yourselves out."

"I'll cut off your hooker money," Player says.

"Shut your mouth," Sid responds almost involuntarily. He actually surprises himself. The Player knew exactly where to hit him and make it count. Without hooker money, Sid will have to spend inordinate amounts of time enticing women into sex with him, if that's even possible. He could steal cash, of course, but cash is hard to steal in large enough quantities to afford acceptable hookers. Fine escorts like Sapphire don't come cheap. He would likely have to settle for street walkers. He has seen the local street walkers . . .

"Fine," Sid caves after a moment's consideration. "Pack up the van. I'll go wake up Sapphire."

# EXT. THE HIGH DESERT - NIGHT

The studio where the Conspiratalk signal originates is surprisingly low key. Some might argue it is less than that. Shoebox-sized may even be an adequate description. Sid had expected a colossal space-age building with many floors and tiers of workers all supporting the gargantuan nationally syndicated media entity, but now he looks up from the front passenger's window of the van and finds that he has to look back down because he overshot the tiny building's rooftop. *Building* may actually be the incorrect nomenclature. Shack or hovel seem more appropriate words to describe the square brick structure with white drapery tightly packed into its old store front window. The window indicates it must have been a small shop once, in decades past, and that was repurposed on the cheap. A heavy black iron gate bars the front entrance next to the window. Above it, a neon sign glows red in the darkness, notifying everyone within sight that the show is On Air.

"When you said he has ten million listeners a week I figured the place would be bigger," Sid says. They have made certain that is not the case. They circled the building twice, counting the exits and looking for escape routes, which are both plentiful and scarce depending on perspective. The building sits by itself on a desert road with the nearest landmark being a small group of trailers a quarter mile away. So while there are technically limitless directions to run, there are exactly none that provide a covered escape—the only kind of escape that matters.

Though Bart Gong's voice is somewhat sporadic, his guest has been prattling on for no less than the last thirty seconds without stopping for air. His name is Tom Danielewski and he has written a book about a secret underground base in Dulce New Mexico which he believes is ninety levels deep and houses contingents of reptilian humanoids who are working with the United States Air Force toward some unknown sinister goal. Gong finally breaks in with a "that's interesting," as if simply to signify his presence in the room for anyone who might have forgotten what they were listening to.

"Alright," Sid says, racking the slide of a suppressed FNX-45 and reaching for the door handle.

"Hold up, man," Bruce cautions. "Let's at least wait for him to go to commercial. You want the whole country to hear us busting in there?"

"Fine." Sid holsters his FNX under his shoulder and rests against the door as they wait for Bart to cut into his guest's ceaseless nonsense and announce a break for sponsors.

The reptilians come from a planet called Alpha Draconis in the Draconis system. They are the ultimate puppet masters over mankind, and they're trying to build a society where they sit at the top of these sort of monarch over all of us and humanity is-it's enslaved-mentally within the matrix, to fight wars for them and project the negative energies back to their moon base for harvesting. These creatures aren't physically feeding on human beings. They're feeding on our negative energy. They subsist on feelings of fear and hate which they absorb psychically.

"False," Sid declares.

Mary Sue leans in from the back of the van. "Which part?" she timidly asks.

"All of it. The reptilians don't control the Order. The Order hates them. They don't feed on negative energy. They literally eat people. They're not from another planet. They're from the fourth dimension."

"You've seen lizard people?"

It's time for us to go to a commercial. Stay tuned and when we come back, more with Danielewski on Dulce Base.

"Let's do this," Sid grunts as he pushes through the van door and stomps toward the radio studio's gated entrance. The others are unprepared to keep up with him. They're still in the van as he blasts through the gate lock with the FNX's entire magazine and rips the gate open to get at the door beyond it. He stomp kicks the door, causing the latch and bolt to skip from their strike plate and swing into the cramped space beyond.

Inside the radio studio, a small beer-gutted man with a thick horseshoe mustache and his head enveloped by a hefty looking pair of headphones sits alone behind a three-sectioned desk packed with computer monitors and many microphones. The workspace takes up most of the room, leaving only a tight walking space between it and the wall all the way around, so Sid goes over the desk, tramping on cables and keyboards, kicking at least one arm-mounted condenser mic out of his way on the path to Gong.

The radio show host is too bewildered to do anything but pitch back in his seat as Sid points the FNX at his nose and barks "I want your call records."

"Take whatever you want," Gong says. The boxy FNX suppressor bobs along to follow his nose as he speaks. "This is just an entertainment program. We don't want any trouble."

Gong's tone is too flat to be genuine, and Sid reads his rigid eyes as a sure sign the man is trying not to look at something. He plants a foot on Gong's chest and kicks him away from the desk. Gong barrels over his chair backward and Sid feels under the lip of the desk to find a sawed-off shotgun, double barreled. It was affixed there with a strip of leather riveted to one of the desk's aluminum crossbars. The radio host was stalling for a chance to reach for the gun. Commendable. Sid might have done the same, but he would have been better at selling it.

"Nice," Sid says as he breaks open the shotgun and lets the shells fall to the floor in front of Gong. "Not a sound plan though. You've got a gate that will keep out the average crackhead, which means anybody coming through that door will be well equipped, maybe a tactical team or something. So a one-off weapon like this will be worth fuck all, especially if they have body armor. You might want to look into a subgun. An uzi maybe. I prefer a P90 for stuff like this because the 5.7 has a little better armor piercing capability."

"Who are you?" Gong says.

"I'm Kill Team One," Sid informs him matter-of-factly. "The real one."

"I don't know anything," Gong says in a panicked whisper. "This is just an entertainment program."

"Duh." Sid rolls his eyes. "You guys are wrong about all this stuff. And that Danielewski guy is a clown. Where can I see the call logs?"

Bruce enters the studio with Mary Sue, the two of them just now catching up, and he seems terribly unhappy with what he sees. "Aw come on, man! You can't just smack Bart Gong around! We don't got to wreck the place!"

"What was I supposed to do?" Sid counters. "Oh hi, Mr. Gong, I can't tell you who I am, but I really need your call logs. I can't say why either. Kay, bye."

"Who are you people?" Bart Gong remains on the floor. His headset dangles at the end of its line over the edge of the desk at Sid's back. It ended up there when it was ripped from Gong's head after Sid kicked him end over end. Tom Danielewski's confused questions coming through as unintelligibly low-volume bits of static from the swinging cans.

"Mr. Gong," Bruce says. "I'm a huge fan. I've been listening for years. Really sorry about all this."

Mary Sue purses her lips, uncertain what to make of Bruce's display, then sets to work at one of the studio's workstations.

"I don't want any trouble," Bart Gong says, now braced against the bottom of the rear studio wall. "You can be Kill Team One. You can be whoever you want. Take whatever you want."

"Is there anybody else in here?" Sid asks, looking around the room, and through a glass partition over Gong's head into the only other room in the building, a small booth containing a chair and sound mixing board.

"No. Nobody else. Just take what you want and leave."

Sid looks to Bruce incredulously.

"He's telling the truth," Bruce says. "Bart produces the show all by himself. He doesn't even have a call screener."

"I have the number," Mary Sue says as she begins scrolling through whatever electronic directory she has loaded on her cell phone. "It looks like the call came from a payphone in Chicago."

"Chicago, Illinois?" Sid asks.

"No, the other Chicago," Bruce heckles.

Sid has been to Chicago. He spent some time there during his last days working for Graveyard. He does not like that city, though his reasons are not at all concrete and might even be downright nebulous. "I hate Chicago."

"You hate everything."

Bart Gong has apparently come back to a crescendo in the waveform that is his nerve, and he eyes Sid with tenacity he seemed incapable of in the cowering moments between reaching for a shotgun and begging on the floor. "If you're really Kill Team One, tell me why you were at the Morston Mall Massacre."

"Easy. To stop a psychopath from stealing a dimension ripping doomsday weapon. I killed him. Also, the terrorists that blew up the city a few months later were trying to kill me. They work for the 12th Imam. He's real. And I shot all those people at Wendigo Joe's casino, but they were possessed by a communist nanovirus that controlled their minds so I kinda had to."

"You can't tell him all this stuff!" Mary Sue squawks.

"Why not? Nobody will believe him. I'll throw in some garbage too. Vampires are real. 9/11 was an inside job. A woman can do anything a man can do. That big school shooting last year was a hoax. Which one of those things is true? Trick question. They're all false. Or are they?"

"I can do anything a man can do," Mary Sue says.

"Yeah? Can you slap a mob boss's daughter in the face with your dick?"

Mary Sue frowns. "That's gross."

"I'm real sorry, Mr. Gong," Bruce says. "He was raised by a guy who was raised by wolves."

"Yeah. Did you know I'm actually Kill Team One Two? There was another one before me. That's exclusive." He finds a nearby microphone and speaks directly into it. "You heard it here first!"

"That mic is off," Bart manages, seemingly now too bewildered to do more than lie on the floor very still, shifting his eyes between the others like a man encased in a statue.

"Shit." Sid shrugs. "Well whatever. We got what we need. Interview's over. Hashtag rapid dominance. Tweet that out on your twit box. And come see me in actual real ultraviolence, opening this Friday. It's gonna be the biggest movie of the year."

"How much TV have you been watching?" Bruce asks as Sid saunters past him for the door. Mary Sue jumps up from her seat and comes with them.

"A lot."

# INT. UTILITY VAN - DAY

It took the Player only about fifteen minutes to look back at the location of the payphone attached to that number at the time stamp of the call to the Conspiratalk show and then follow the caller to his current whereabouts. During the call, Jamie, if that is his real name, was interrupted by heavily armed agents of some unknown and unofficial entity. He was taken to a building on the outskirts of Chicago by three men wearing body armor and toting XM8 rifles. The rifles were the first sure evidence that something serious is going on with this Jamie guy. Those guns are oddities. Gang bangers definitely wouldn't have them. XM8s were designed as military prototypes in the 1990s but never adopted by the United States army. As such, they were never very widely disseminated, and other newer rifles greatly surpassed them in proliferation.

One of those newer rifles is Sid's current go-to for shootouts, assassinations, and all his other favorite forms of anti-social behavior: the HK416. He and Bruce recently picked up a case of them from Bruce's contacts in the Devil's Undertakers motorcycle gang. The German manufactured Heckler and Koch HK416 platform is a gas-operated battle rifle based on the ArmaLite AR-15 design and equipped with a short-stroke piston to reduce malfunctions more common to the direct impingement system utilized by standard AR-15 variants. Sid attached vertical foregrips and red dot optics to all of the rifles.

"How many are there?" Sid says.

"I've counted at least eight moving in and out of the house in the last twenty four hours," Player informs him. "Unfortunately, they've been in the city too long to trace back a point of origin on the video." The Player refers to the 800 trillion megapixel spy satellite which he uses to record everything that happens in the continental United States—but only for the last seven days. Video recorded at such ludicrous resolution requires equally ludicrous amounts of storage media. The week of footage Player normally keeps purportedly fills a jumbo jet hangar, though Sid has never seen it himself.

"If they have hardware like that, they're not amateurs."

"There were no guns used in any of the previous murders," Mary Sue says.

"I noticed."

"Why do you think they kidnapped the caller this time, but killed all the others?"

"It's not the killer that grabbed him," Bruce says. He's stating the conclusion he and Sid already reached. "There's somebody else in the game."

"You know there's still time to abort this mess," Sid suggests. "We could be back at the firehouse in a couple hours. Get some Chinese takeout? Maybe check out a movie? I've been meaning to watch *Universal Soldier*. That's a good one, right?"

Player shuts him down with two words. "Sid. No."

"Fuck," Sid grumbles. It was a long shot, but he figured he would try. He really needs to learn to talk to girls. Then Player won't have anything to hang over him anymore. "I hate all of you."

"Come on, man," Bruce coaxes. "This thing should be some easy shit. Probably turn out to be nothing. We're talking about journalists here. They probably got a story some fat cat wants to kill and that's all it is. Shit happens all the time."

"Either way, I'm trying out the dread suit." Sid's words cause Mary Sue's face to light up with enthusiasm, then frustration.

"It's called the Panoply of Freedom," she insists.

"That's a stupid name. Dread suit." This has been an ongoing argument for the last three weeks, since Mary Sue started measuring him for the custom battle armor that Sid is currently pulling from a crate at the rear of the van.

After the fight with Red Ghoul at the Brunswick family farm did not go smoothly, Player suggested Sid equip himself with better protective gear besides the occasional flak vest. The reasoning was not difficult to work through considering his history. Enemies of all kinds have fired approximately a billion bullets at Sid Hansen in his lifetime. None of them has ever hit him. In the meantime, he has been beaten, blown up, stabbed, sliced, shadow kicked, twisted, bitten and trampled. All of this prompted the Player's assertion that maybe protection from bullets isn't really what Sid needs.

The dread suit is a form-fitting set of shirt, pants, boots, helmet, and gloves, all made from stitched-together Kevlar with Kydex plates covering all the vital non-moving areas. The plates are padded with a layer of foam and vaguely imply the form of a muscle bound human male-but only if shining a 5000-watt spotlight on the damn thing. Mary Sue sprayed the whole suit with some kind of cutting-edge ultra-matte black enamel which absorbs 99.8% of visible light. Sid tried the suit on twice for fitting, and both times found his appearance in a mirror unsettling. He looks like a shadow. With the helmet off, he looks kind of like a disembodied head floating over a silhouette. His body has no definition and appears two-dimensional under all but the brightest direct light. Mary Sue explained that the lack of definition would make it harder for attackers to see the joints in the armor and aim for them.

"I still think it should be bulletproof," he says, removing his well-worn blue jeans while staring boldly at Mary Sue. She exaggeratedly averts her gaze. Sid grins.

"It would be too heavy if it was bullet resistant," Mary Sue says, now shielding her eyes with a cupped hand. "Besides, you're impervious to bullets anyway."

"That's not true. I'm just good at utilizing cover."

"Well, bullets never hit you either way, so we decided to focus on close-up threats. You should be pretty well protected from any blunt force trauma, slashing weapons, concussive blasts—it's really a lot more like a suit of medieval armor than modern body armor."

"So it's already obsolete? Great."

They didn't completely ignore his input for the suit design though. There are two features which Sid won out on. One is the skull-faced silicon carbide helmet. If you're going to have a helmet, it might as well be scary. That's self-explanatory. The other feature is the gloves, more accurately gauntlets, which are plated to a ridiculously intricate degree. His fingers are braced with titanium rods and each individual phalanx has its own carbide shield. This is because hands are more important, and more delicate, than most people ever think about. Also, Sid has always wanted to punch somebody in the face with a metal glove.

"When we get there," Bruce says. "I'm gonna go in first. Knock on the door, see if I can settle things the civil way."

"I don't think that's a good idea," Sid says.

"Neither is you crashing in there and mowing everybody down. We don't know who these people are. They might be on our side."

"I think you're crazy."

"Crazy like a fox."

"What?" Sid challenges the last statement. "What does that mean? Are you agreeing with me?"

"No. I'm saying I'm crazy like a fox. That's an expression."

"I've never heard that. You're full of shit."

"Nah. Mary Sue, isn't that a thing? Crazy like a fox."

"Yes, I think so," Mary Sue says. "You're crazy, but you're crazy in a good way."

"No one says that," Sid argues. "You two are making this up."

"People say that shit, man," Bruce insists.

"Well you're gonna get killed in there."

"I think you're underestimating my smooth talking skills."

## INT. RENTAL PROPERTY - DAY

Bruce Freeman is currently zip tied to a chair. It's a nice chair, not padded or anything, just finished wood, but nice looking. He has been tied to much more rickety chairs before. A gaggle of men surround him, hovering with contempt and flak jackets. Some of them have guns. One of them is demanding answers.

Bruce really overestimated his smooth talking skills.

The house is a two-story on the South Side—too clean to be abandoned, but too devoid of furniture and trappings to be lived in. The whole place is empty except for a few sleeping bags and chairs. Bruce's guess is these guys are squatting here, or rented the joint short term with cash and no names. Both are accepted practices in the spy biz.

"Who are you?" says the leader of the group, blasting a mag light in Bruce's eyes from only inches away. He's a husky character, with a well-trimmed beard and beady little eyes under an animated unibrow. As big as he is, his pants are clearly a few sizes too big for him, and kept up by a set of drab suspenders that blend in with the rest of his tactical gear. It's an odd detail. These mercenary types don't generally wear baggy clothes. Stuff like that is a life threatening hazard in a firefight.

"It's like four PM," Bruce says, in no way intimidated by the light in his eyes in the already brightly lit room. "What's with the mag light?"

"I ask the questions here!"

"Yeah. Everybody says that when they got you tied to a chair. It's a cliché, man. You gotta have a give and take, you know? Any kind of conversation has to go both ways."

"This isn't a conversation." The commando team leader sounds like he's probably from the Midwest, definitely American—not an import mercenary. "It's an interrogation."

"Man, I don't want to get into semantics. I'm gonna level with you. I'm here with this major badass motherfucker. . ."

"Kill Team One?" The interrogator snaps at the mention without letting Bruce finish. Apparently these guys are already acquainted. "What does the kill team want with Chan?"

"Chan? Look, right now, Kill Team One is right outside, and if you guys don't get real cool in the next minute, he's gonna bust in here and kill everybody. All y'all motherfuckers. I'm trying to prevent that from happening. I'm a peace broker. I'm a ambassador right now."

One of the other bag men speaks up. "Shut up," he yells in Bruce's face, his breath smelling strongly of salami and onions, then whips his attention back to the leader. "This guy's yanking your dick, Fleabag."

"That is a really weird nickname," Bruce remarks. It is. It's the kind of nickname that has to have spawned from a great story. Maybe he got fleas from an ex-girlfriend, or he sleeps in a doghouse because his wife snores. Whatever it is, it lends credence to the theory that these guys are real spooks and not just some mob goons. Real operators tend to have the kind of nicknames cruel kids put upon each other in middle school. It's never Nighthawk, or Eagle Talon. It's always stuff like Gooch or Pedobear. "And I'm totally serious here. You guys are possibly just seconds away from a whirling vortex of death and destruction. I mean some biblical shit. Weeping and gnashing teeth type shit."

"If you're telling the truth, then why didn't he just come in here himself?" says salami breath.

As if to answer his question, a wall on the far side of the room explodes into chalky white dust and chunks of drywall, causing Bruce and most of the goons to avert their eyes. Sid steps through the gaping hole onto the ugly orange carpet of the wide open living room. He looks like a spectre of death, a man-shaped shadow with a glaring grey skull and scary black rifle. The guns and grenades and the straps securing them to his body have the definition that the rest of him does not, causing them to appear like 3-dimensional objects attached to a 2-dimensional form. Sid points the rifle at Bruce's captors and all of the men go leaping for cover, some of them into an adjoining room and others over an island counter behind Bruce's chair.

"Shit, motherfucker," Bruce says. "How many breaching charges did you use?"

"Four," Sid shrugs. "We have more."

Someone holds a Glock 17 around the corner from the adjoining room and squeezes off two blind suppressing shots before Sid zeros on his location. The kill team fires only once and nails the hostile shooter through the wall.

"Shit!" somebody shouts. "Fleabag is down!"

"Fucker's the real deal! Abort! Abort!"

Bruce watches with a look of incredulity as men barrel back over the kitchen counter and into the next room. One guy leaps through a window to get away, doubtlessly cutting himself in the rain of broken glass that showers his body. Bruce leans back in the chair to get a better view into the adjoining room just in time to see two commandos crash into each other on their way through a door frame in their panicked haste to escape the house.

"Come on, cocksuckers! Nobody wants to party?" Sid shouts after them. After he receives no answer, and all of the men have cleared the house, Sid lets his rifle hang from its strap. He whips a KA-BAR knife from a sheath on his chest to cut Bruce free from the half dozen zip ties the commandos used to strap him to the chair. "That was even easier than I figured it would be."

"We didn't get Chan-the guy from the phone call," Bruce says, rubbing one of his wrists after Sid freed it from the overly tight plastic ties.

"There's somebody upstairs," Sid says. "I heard him stomping around."

"How do you hear anything after those breach charges?" Bruce complains, definitely still experiencing ringing in his ears from when Sid blasted the wall down. He does hear something though. He hears the shuffling of another person in the room, prompting him to look over his shoulder and spot the bloody carcass of Fleabag being flopped by someone onto the hardwood kitchen floor nearby. Then he realizes there is no one else there to move the body. Then he realizes the body is moving on its own.

Fleabag props his torso up on one elbow and glares up at them. Blood gushes from the bullet hole in the side of his head as he growls angrily. His beard seems heavier now—there's actually a lot more hair on his face. His teeth sprout into gargantuan fangs.

"What the fuck, man?!" Bruce screams like a school girl. "What the fuck?!"

"We didn't happen to pack silver bullets in the van, did we?" Sid asks, as the hulking man-wolf rises from the floor on its tree trunk legs, stooping to avoid hitting its head on the ceiling. He has to already know the answer.

"No," Bruce says. The kill team groans loudly.

"Find Chan. I'll fight the werewolf."

# INT. RENTAL PROPERTY - DAY

Fleabag, the werewolf, is a massive beast with bulging muscles and claws long as steak knives. It's a man shaped thing, except for its legs, which have an extra joint like a dog's hind legs, and its head, which is very much a snouted wolf-head. Its ears are also unusually tall and pointed, almost bat-like, a detail which sticks out as peculiar to Sid, but very well may be common among werewolves. He has only seen one other before and can't be sure that one wasn't the exception.

Before the monster can do anything at all, Sid does the only thing that makes sense. He lights it the fuck up.

There's something oddly comforting about firing a fully automatic weapon. Suppressive fire is so called because it suppresses enemy maneuvers and return fire, but Sid feels like it suppresses more than that. It suppresses problems—especially at a range so short that all of the bullets are going directly into said problem. The M4 thunders in Sid's hands as the bolt carrier pumps and the extractor whips a steady stream of shell casings from the right side of the rifle onto the hard wood.

A half dozen 200-grain bullets slam into the monster's teeth as it bucks wildly to avoid the gunfire. The monster's fangs break like fallen china and tumble onto the countertop beside it. A few rounds end up in the walls, but most of the magazine gets buried in the werewolf's sinewy chest before it bounds off the kitchen counter and leaps at Sid with its arms outstretched in a massive belly flopping tackle. Sid drops the rifle and rolls toward the sailing monster, slipping beneath its clawed feet and drawing his KA-BAR as he hops up from the floor.

It's a good knife, but it isn't going to do a whole lot of good. Werewolves regenerate very quickly and are virtually impossible to kill with conventional weapons. Their particular brand of regeneration does not work to repair wounds caused by silver objects, which affect them just like normal weapons affect normal creatures. Sid killed the last werewolf he encountered by fashioning a shiv from a broken toothbrush and dipping it in molten silver before stabbing the thing in the eye. Unfortunately, none of those implements appear to be available here.

Sid weaves under wicked swiping talons and stabs the monster in the guts twice, then uppercuts it in the jaw. To his surprise, the werewolf reels away from the impact of his punch, then backs off and glares at him cautiously. For a fraction of a second, Sid is as confused as the monster. It's the gauntlets. He always wanted to punch a guy in the face with metal gloves, but their utility for fighting even bigger things never even crossed his mind until now. Sid fakes a left jab and the werewolf actually flinches.

"Ha! You flinched!" he shouts.

The werewolf snorts and forces out a heavily distorted "Fuck you."

"I enjoy doggie style," Sid says. The monster immediately turns tail and runs, tearing off down a hallway deeper into the house and leaving Sid standing in the kitchen gloating to himself. He just won a boxing match with a werewolf. He shouts after the monster as he heads down the hallway to seek it out. "Maybe if you have a sister or something. . ."

That is when Sid hears the unmistakable and all too familiar sound of an M134 minigun's rotary barrels spinning up. He throws himself to the floor just as a flickering beam of hot lead chops through the wall beside him like an invisible chainsaw. That gun expels bullets so fast and with such velocity that the werewolf firing it in this flimsy wooden house is akin to swinging around an 800 foot long lightsaber. A curtain of strafing gunfire extends over Sid's head and he experiences a microsecond of deja vu. This is actually not the first time a werewolf has tried to kill him with a rotary gun.

Sid slides his knife back into its sheath and draws his FNX-45s as he crawls along the hallway. The dread suit has plated and padded elbows, which is great for rolling and worming across twenty feet of drywall pebbles and wood splinters that used to be walls. The minigun is very quickly tearing the house apart.

Reaching the door to the room from which the god-slaughtering storm of 7.62x51mm bullet-death is coming, Sid stops and waits without showing himself. If he just runs in there, the werewolf will turn the bullet hose on him. That's the last thing he needs. Despite Mary Sue and Lily Hoffman's absurd ideas, bullets do not just go around him. He tries to formulate a better plan.

A minigun like that eats ammunition faster than most people can comprehend. Even a gunship generally only carries enough ammo for ten to twenty seconds of continuous fire. Unless the werewolf has a shipping crate of cartridges in there, the gun is going to run dry in a few seconds. The problem is that the house might collapse before that happens.

# INT. RENTAL PROPERTY - UPSTAIRS - DAY

Upstairs in the rental property, Bruce creeps along a carpeted hallway, covering his ears with his hands to try and muffle some of the earth-shaking belch of what he can only guess is some kind of electrically powered machine gun. It sounds more like a roar than the rhythmic blasting that normally comes to mind when thinking of a machine gun, and this particular roar would belong to something much larger than any North American land animal.

Bruce lost his gun somewhere downstairs. The assholes who grabbed him at the front door took it when they searched him, and he didn't have time to go searching for it when Sid cut him loose and began a boxing match with a five-hundred pound wolfman. Now Bruce is just hoping he can find their boy Jamie and get out of here without running into some commando badass or getting perforated by an artillery piece.

He stops creeping and starts running, because attempting to muffle his footfalls suddenly seems pointless when the noise level from just down the stairs well exceeds that of a Cannibal Corpse concert. He peeks in two open doorways to completely empty rooms on his way to a closed door at the end of the hall. He tries the knob and realizes it is already moving, something made imperceptible until he touched it, due to the vibrations and noise from below. The knob won't turn, but it is definitely jiggling. That's really strange to Bruce until he notices the little protruding latch set in the middle of the knob and the screws on either side affixing the knob to the door. All of those parts should be on the other side of the door. The commando goons must have taken the knob apart and reversed it to lock from the outside. It's a cute idea, but it wouldn't be any way to keep Bruce prisoner, and Sid would find it downright laughable. The door is flimsy hollow pressboard. They would just go through it.

Bruce undoes the latch and the door flies backward, yanked open with terrified ferocity. Someone slams into him a fraction of a second later, but rebounds back to the carpeted floor of the bedroom beyond. He looks down into the frightened eyes of the person who was locked inside.

# INT. RENTAL PROPERTY - DOWNSTAIRS - DAY

Pinned down on the carpet by relentless gunfire, Sid Hansen looks up at the uneven trails off bullet holes carved in the hallway wall above him and comes up with an idea that seems like it should have been a total no-brainer. He rises to his knees, takes a quick glance through one of the holes, just long enough to make out the huge werewolf on the others side, its drooling jaws hanging open as it blasts away with the minigun in wide sweeping swaths. Sid drives the muzzle of his FNX into another bullet hole, the threaded barrel making a neat peg to fit the ragged opening in the drywall. He then fires a single shot into a black cylindrical housing attached to the minigun's body. This is the disconnector, the mechanism which frees each fresh cartridge in the belt from its metal linking and feeds it to the whirling set of chambers beyond, to be fired down one of the six rotating barrels. With the disconnector broken, the spinning barrels grind to a halt. The gun's motor whirrs loudly as it strains to push through the knot of linked ammo now jammed up in the system.

The werewolf looks to his belt of ammunition, his yellow wolf eyes following it down to the big ammo can beside him, a black box about the size of the average duffel bag, and which Sid knows to have a capacity of 1000 rounds. The werewolf looks back up at the gun. He could not have heard Sid's shot over all the noise, but now he sees the cracked housing where a .45 ACP round wrecked his gun and he howls with rage.

Sid bounds into the doorway and blasts the werewolf with the full fury of both FNX pistols. The werewolf hurls the forty pound minigun at Sid, but aims poorly in its frustration and hits the wall beside him. The gun impacts so hard it actually sinks into the drywall. Sid doesn't have time to marvel at that as he dodges a flurry of talon swipes from the monster. Its claws are four inches long, making it a wonder the thing could even operate that gun without them getting in the way.

The werewolf snaps at his neck, and Sid bobs and back peddles to avoid its terrifying jaws. He whips it across the teeth with a pistol, then jams his KA-BAR into its chin, pinning the monster's bottom jaw to the top. The werewolf reels dizzily, then leans against a nearby wall. The wall, already badly shredded by automatic weapons fire, collapses under the monster's substantial weight. The werewolf falls through, ending up back in the room adjoining the kitchen—the same room where the fight started.

"Come on, man," Sid says. "You're getting wrecked here." He steps through the massive jagged opening in the drywall to gloat over the fallen monster as it rips the KA-BAR from its chin. "What do you think is gonna happen?"

The massive beast lashes at Sid's ankle with a hand like a bear trap, but Sid hops away to avoid the flailing hand. The werewolf is up then, surprisingly quickly. It rushes him down, snarling and barking as Sid blasts away with both pistols. The monster compresses its legs to pounce, which Sid ducks to avoid, but the werewolf never leaves the ground. Instead, it grabs him by the arms. That werewolf learns quickly.

The monster is incredibly strong. It is twice Sid's size, and Sid is by no means small. Sid isn't going to beat this thing in a wrestling match. He empties both pistols into its eyes, then smashes his boot toe into its chin and snakes both arms over the werewolf's hands to break the monster's grip at the thumbs. He leaps back as the beast howls in pain.

Sid reloads his guns. He's exploring alternatives for finishing this fight off. He could light the werewolf on fire somehow. Werewolves hate fire. It won't kill them, but they heal from burns slowly. If he had a bigger cutting weapon he could hack off its head. That does the trick with werewolves too, but the big bastard isn't going to sit still while he saws its head off with a combat knife.

Then Mary Sue drives a van into the house and makes things easier. The grill of the GMC utility van smashes through the wall, sending brick and foam insulation avalanching into the kitchen. The werewolf vanishes under the front bumper like a swimmer chomped down by megalodon.

Bruce pokes his head through the passenger's side window as the vehicle comes to a stop. "I'll huff and I'll puff and I'll blow *your* house down, asshole."

"You know he's not dead right?" Sid dryly explains, spoiling the fun of Bruce's moment. He can't be sure if Bruce knows these things. Supernatural creatures were not his focus in the CIA. "Not unless that van has a silver bumper."

Bruce only smirks in sheer disregard for any threat the monster might pose. "Whatever. Get in, loser," he yells. He tears back the sliding van door, knocking loose some debris from the debris pile, and Sid hops up into the vehicle to meet Jamie.

# INT. UTILITY VAN - DAY

Jamie is a small Asian person on the floor of Sid's van. Jamie skids around the hard plastic floor as Mary Sue guns the engine and reverses the van out of the broken house.

"Watch for Fleabag. We don't want to take another super monster for a ride." Bruce is of course referring to the time a member of the collective sentience known as Red Scare hitched a ride in the trunk of his car, possessed the Ghoul, and nearly killed Sid in an old farmhouse. Bruce points out the writhing form of the werewolf in the rubble they left behind and declares "We're good. Go!"

"Everybody hold on!" Mary Sue shrieks, pounding down the gas and whipping the van around onto the street in front of the crumbling rental house in a perfect Rockford turn. Jamie screams like a schoolgirl as the vehicle spins.

"Head downtown," Bruce says, climbing into the front of the van to sit in the passenger's seat again as the van accelerates on the straightaway ahead of them. "It's the middle of the day. Graveyard isn't gonna do shit in front of all them eyes."

"Are you sure it was Graveyard?" Mary Sue asks, screeching the van around a corner. She almost immediately jerks the wheel again and takes them around another corner. She's doing a textbook maneuver to lose anyone who might be tailing them, especially in a city grid like this one. Turn down a street, move laterally, repeat.

"With that kinda hardware and a werewolf right here in Chi-town? Bet your ass." This is a logical assumption. Not many organizations have access to gear like that *and* creatures of the night *and* can get them both into the country.

Sid studies the strange visual enigma known as Jamie silently as he processes the details of their situation. Determining his business with the werewolf and the house has concluded, and that they have a planned destination, he then devotes the full focus of his mental faculties to the person on the floor.

Sid can't decipher if Jamie's eastern, and therefore unfamiliar, features are somehow hampering his sense for human forms, or if Jamie is actually not a normal human in a way that is observable to everyone. The little person is clothed in baggy cargo pants and a tight-fitting t-shirt that covers a waifish figure. If Jamie is something truly alien, that would explain a lot about why such powerful forces are looking for him.

"What are you?" Sid says, leaning in for a closer look. He observes the lack of whiskers on Jamie's baby-smooth face, the crisp lines of Jamie's ultra-short haircut—unusually clean for the circumstances.

"What do you mean?" Jamie whines. "Who are you people? Where are you taking me?"

"I think he wants to know if you're a dude or a chick," Bruce cuts in over the seatback. "Or trans or something."

"I'm non-binary."

"Shit, that wasn't A or B or C."

"A shapeshifter," Sid concludes. "I've met one of these before. They're extremely dangerous." He plants a palm on the grip of an FNX.

"Huh?" Jamie worriedly squeaks.

"It ain't like that, Sid," Bruce says. "This is just some weird liberal gay shit, not weird space alien from another dimension shit."

"I think you guys are being mean to Jamie," Mary Sue chirps back at them. "Not everyone identifies as strictly male or strictly female. Some people have fluid concepts of their gender."

"The whole world's gone crazy," Bruce mutters. None of these answers are satisfactory to Sid, who still cannot determine the sex of this strange being. He rises up over Jamie, raising the dread gauntlets with outstretched fingers and grim determination as a look of fear spreads across the sexless creature's face.

"I need to see if it has a penis or a vagina," Sid says.

Bruce reacts with a panicky quickness, reaching over the seatback and grabbing hold of Sid's left bicep to prevent any forceful examinations. "No-no-no-no-no! Don't do that! I already got enough shit I wish I could erase from my brain 'cause of you. I don't need that!"

Sid rests back against the wall of the van and snorts angrily at Bruce. "Fine, but if this thing turns into a giant amorphous blob and asphyxiates us all, it's on you."

"What do we do if we run into that werewolf again?" Mary Sue asks.

"We're gonna get some silver," Sid says.

"How do we do that?"

# INT. TIFFANY & CO - DAY

Sid yanks open the front door with a vengeance and stomps into Tiffany & Co like he's entering a professional wrestling ring. He glances left, to a counter display of diamond necklaces and two well-dressed women inspecting them, right to another counter containing hundreds of diamond rings, then straight ahead to a woman in a skirt suit who is eyeballing him with an apprehension markedly above what he normally draws from store clerks (and it should be noted that Sid commonly inspires exceptional apprehension in store clerks).

"Silver bullets," Sid barks. He is still wearing the dread suit, although Bruce convinced him to cover it up with some baggy sweatpants and an old bomber jacket he had stashed in the back of the van. He left the helmet in the van. Otherwise this place would already be erupting in panic.

The clerk, to her credit, doesn't even stutter. She's a rosy cheeked thing, short, blond, big-breasted by Sid's estimate, although her fuzzy sweater hardly accentuates that feature. She skips the usual pleasantries and goes right to answering his question with a high pitch and drawn out annunciation of uncertainty. "Silver bullets? Like for vampires?"

"Werewolves," Sid says. "Vampires aren't real."

"We don't sell bullets here. Sorry." She purses her lips to the left side in a gesture of apology that is ambiguously genuine or facetious.

"Then I just need whatever silver stuff you have."

"Okay. Are you looking for rings? Necklaces?"

"Whatever has the most silver," Sid says.

"Oh, right." The jewelry girl laughs. "Okay. Well, there are some bracelets over here. They would have the most actual silver, I guess." She directs Sid to a display case containing rows of bracelets cast in silver and gold, with a variety of gemstones inlaid in diverse patterns.

"Great." Sid eyes the bracelets and points to several that have few or no stones attached, as those will just get in the way later. "I want that one, that one, that one, and that one. Bag them up." He reaches into the side pocket of the bomber jacket and makes a withdrawal of a crisp new hundred dollar bill, which he slaps down on the glass countertop confidently. "Keep the change."

Now the jewelry girl does stutter. "I . . .um . . . I don't think that will quite cover it."

"That's a hundred dollars," Sid reestablishes, jabbing curiously at the bill with his index finger.

"Yes. And just this one bracelet is five hundred dollars."

"What!?" Sid shouts, loud enough to turn heads around the store. A man sitting by the diamond ring display pays him a particularly nasty look. "Seriously?"

Silence stretches for a few seconds before the jewelry girl decides his question was posed in sincerity, at least enough to warrant an answer. "Yes," she says.

"But it doesn't do anything."

"It's pretty."

The jewelry *girl* is very pretty. The *jewelry* is functionless metal. Sid can assign only a cursory value to it for its use as a decoration. It is worth as much as a napkin used to scribble on out of boredom, or a sign advertising some entertainment product, but not a sign conveying any sort of useful information like directions or a warning. Those types of signs have value. These trinkets do not. They are beneath toilet paper in the hierarchy of Sid's values, because toilet paper can be used to wipe his ass, while a bracelet cannot.

"Well," Sid grumbles as he stretches open his wallet and yanks the rest of the money from inside. He slaps it down on the counter and fans out the bills. Eight hundred dollars. "Just give me whatever this will buy."

"Okay." Jewelry girl starts ringing up bracelets while Sid leans on the counter.

"You know where I can get a butane torch, a graphite crucible, and a bag of sand?"

The question compels the jewelry girl to look at Sid like he's a talking dog made of cheese. She shakes her head.

"Power tools," he simplifies. "Where can I get power tools?"

"Um . . . there's a Home Depot behind the Best Buy on Roosevelt."

# INT. BLACK VAN - DAY

Sid returns to the boxy black utility van to find Bruce has switched places with Mary Sue. The spy hunter is now at the steering wheel holding a massive hot dog, one smothered in relish, tomatoes, mustard, and pickles. He practically has to unhinge his jaw to fit the end of the monstrosity into his mouth. He stuffs his face with the thing and then says something nearly incomprehensible over Mary Sue and Jamie's heads as Sid climbs into the rear of the van.

"Hey, tell him what you just told us," Bruce says. Only it comes out more like Te hi o wu ja tow us. Jamie doesn't seem to understand. Sid pulls the van doors closed behind him after getting a good look around for prying eyes. The streets are busy with foot traffic, and a good spy will blend in, but not all spies are good ones, so it's always worth a look.

"This is very interesting," Mary Sue explains. She sits with her legs crossed on the floor notably close to Jamie. Their cozy positioning is the beginning of Sid's mental pile of context clues meant to solve the mystery of Jamie's sex. Of course, Mary Sue is a virgin and doesn't seem to express much interest in sex, so maybe there's nothing going on there. This evidence is inconclusive. "Jamie has been filling us in on their situation."

"Whose situation?" Sid asks.

"Theirs," Mary Sue responds very matter-of-factly, as though it was a proper answer and not just a repetition of what prompted the question.

"Who are they?"

"Jamie."

"Right. Who are the other people though?"

"We don't know."

"That's informative." It is not. Sid is no longer sure who they're talking about at all now. Jamie? Him? Graveyard?

"I got us all char dogs," Bruce manages after finally woofing down that walloping mouthful of hot dog. He extends a paper bag to Sid at the end of one arm over the seatback. "There's extra 'cause Mary Sue don't want any."

"Do you know what they put in those things?" Mary Sue questions, though the inflection implies her line is rhetorical. Bruce answers anyway.

"One hundred percent beef, baby. Jews run the Chicago hot dog market. They won't have it no other way." Sid takes the paper bag and begins routing through a pile of crinkle cut fries inside to dig out a foil wrapped hot dog. "Now tell him what you just told us," Bruce says again.

"Kill Team One has tried to kill Jamie twice already in the last two days," Mary Sue says.

"That seems unlikely," Sid reasons. He knows it to be impossible because he has been pounding out a wicked hot milf two states away for the last two days. He didn't try to kill anybody.

"It's true!" Jamie proclaims in a perturbed tone. "He can find me no matter where I go! There's nowhere to hide! He can kill a man just by touching him! Everything they say about him is true!"

"Who says this stuff?" Sid says while peeling back the hot dog foil.

"Conspiracy guys. People on the Data Battles forums. I thought they were just lonely people making up stories for attention. I never heard about any of this until the BuzzWorthy thing and then I did an internet search and it's like the floodgates just opened. I might be the only person who has ever seen Kill Team One and lived to talk about it."

Sid laughs. The implications of that statement, which he has heard before, are staggering. For it to be true he would have to either live in a cave without ever leaving, or just murder every living person he encounters. He would leave a trail of corpses everywhere he goes: big box cashiers, fast food employees, definitely car rental guys, probably some hospital staff, hookers—so many hookers. It would never end. Sid wouldn't have enough bullets for them all.

"But what's he look like?" Bruce says. He smiles, hardly able to contain his amusement. "This is the good part."

"It's not funny!" Jamie shouts. "I know what I saw and I'm not crazy!"

"I didn't say you were." Bruce backs off in his seat, his hands raised in surrender, the hot dog still in one of them. "Just tell him."

Jamie sighs. "Kill Team One is a tall naked man with weird skin and no eyes. He just has empty black spaces where they should be." Jamie pauses briefly before spitting out the next part. "And he can walk through walls."

Sid can't help but shoot a look of skepticism over to Bruce, who shakes his head laughingly. Mary Sue frowns and looks down at the floor as Sid sweeps his eyes over her. He gets the sense she expects him to react badly to this news for some reason, but he can't see why.

"Okay. . ." Sid prods. "Like a ghost?"

"Right through them."

"It explains how all the doors were still locked," Bruce concludes, chuckling quietly.

"I don't think it's possible to phase through solid matter," Mary Sue whispers delicately.

"Ain't possible to turn into a werewolf either."

"It's more complicated than that. I don't think even fringe physics models permit those kinds of interactions."

"I know what I saw," Jamie insists.

Sid has nothing to add regarding the likelihood of a wall-phasing assassin. It has never been his job to understand the hard science behind hostile metahuman abominations or supernatural monsters—only to kill them. "Why does he want you dead?" Sid asks.

"Everyone he . . . killed . . . contributed to the new news division at BuzzWorthy."

Bruce snorts. "That stupid website always pops up on Facebook with Fourteen Things That Prove You Didn't Die Ten Years Ago, or Twenty-Six Celebrities Who Eat Bread?"

"That's the one," Jamie confirms.

"I still can't believe J-Law likes bread!" Mary Sue says. "She's just like us!"

Sid is confused by this development. "They want to kill you because a movie star likes bread?" he says.

"The new news division is strongly social justice oriented." That clears up nothing. "At first I thought we were being targeted by alt-right extremists. We've been doxxed so many times."

"Docked? Docked what now?"

"Doxxed. It's when your real name and address get shared online."

"Because of bread?" Nobody else in the conversation bothers to stop to let Sid catch up.

"No, not for that. We've been doxxed by mostly a bunch of bigots and transphobic white nationalists."

"Can you name anyone specific?" Mary Sue says, already prepared to jot down names in a little notepad.

"Sure. You can start with Rubbernecker. It's a tabloid site we had a spat with a few months ago. They posted nude photos of Brittany Perkins that her ex sold them and they refused to take them down when she asked, so Izzy called them rapists in an editorial and doxxed their editors. Now they're suing the site."

"Oh, that's a good lead," Mary Sue affirms.

"And there's that wrestler Colossal Corey. We posted a sex tape that his mistress sold us and he demanded we take it down. Izzy told him to fuck off. Apparently he never heard of the First Amendment. He's suing the site."

"Okay. That's worth looking at too."

"Who's Izzy?" Bruce asks.

"Izumi Saito," Jamie explains. "My boss. Well, used to be. She started BuzzWorthy straight out of art school with nothing. I mean, her parents gave her a ten million dollar loan, but they expected her to pay it back."

"Damn. Pulled herself up by the bootstraps," Bruce remarks with an eye roll.

"She was really something."

"Did you say something before about white nationalists?" Mary Sue prods.

"Lots. The biggest assholes are PGN. Prestige Global News. It's one of those alt-right fake news sites owned by rich republican fascists. Their main talking head is this miscreant Angus McDougal. He's literally Hitler. He sics his vile fans on us whenever he can."

"Hmmm," Mary Sue sets down her notepad and slides a laptop from under the passenger's seat.

"Don't forget Gamergaters. Nobody is more toxic."

"What kind of toxins do these Gamergaters have?" This could be pertinent later if Sid has to fight them. Poisonous skin can be a tricky exotic weapon, but isn't much more than a speed bump. Nerve gas, or toxic projectiles could be a bigger challenge.

Mary lets out a discouraged squeak. "The comments section on the BuzzWorthy site has a lot of death threats."

"How many death threats?" Bruce says, snickering quietly.

"Um, on this article alone there are four thousand seven hundred sixty two comments, and it looks like most of them are death threats."

"That must be one of the more moderate articles," Jamie says.

"I'm really sorry, but it looks like everybody wants to kill you," Mary Sue whimpers. "This doesn't help at all."

"Wait. Do you think that's who's doing this? Are white nationalists really that tied into the deep state? They're moving past doxxing, trolling, and DDOS attacks to-to this?"

"What the fuck are you talking about?" Sid finally belts out. "Let's go all the way back to the beginning. Who are you?"

Jamie takes a moment of nervous contemplation to rewind and answer Sid's simple question. "I'm Jamie Chan."

"What do you do?"

"I'm an internet blogger. I work for BuzzWorthy."

"And that is?"

"It's an internet content aggregator and news site. We publish editorials, videos and listicles."

"Clickbait," Bruce says.

"Yeah, okay. Clickbait," Jamie begrudgingly agrees. "Every platform has its faults."

"What does that mean?" Sid has never heard this term before.

Bruce answers before Jamie can. "It's stupid lies on the internet that's just supposed to get you to click on it. You see a little headline says they got naked pictures of Ariana Grande but when you click on it you find out it's just sideboob."

"You?" Sid says. "You're responsible for sideboob?"

"No! We do not do sideboob!" Jamie argues.

"What is sideboob?" Mary Sue asks.

"Boob shot in profile. Usually from a 4 o'clock angle," Bruce explains. "Not a nipple to be seen."

Mary Sue reddens with shame. "Oh my."

Sid leers at Jamie with boiling disdain. "You disgust me," he says.

"We don't do that! That's Ogler, or Celeb Jihad. Those sites are total trash."

"So what do you do?"

"We cover a lot of progressive issues, nostalgia, hipster fads, sexism. You ever heard of manhaling? I created that."

"What the hell is manhaling?"

"It's when a woman is on a bus or the subway and there's a man on the bus too, and he's breathing. It's oppressive because that's air that a woman could have breathed."

"That's retarded."

"It got two hundred thousand shares in a day," Jamie beams. "You still think that's retarded?"

"Yes."

"You don't actually believe that manhaling shit?" Bruce asks. "Do you?"

"Of course not. Nobody actually believes it. That's how outrage porn works."

"Outrage porn?"

"An article that's solely written to piss off some segment of the readers. Manhaling is classic outrage porn. Nobody ever really believed in it in the first place, but the article pissed off a bunch of cis male conservatives and they shared it with other cis male conservatives so they could all go flame the site, and the site cashed a fat check from all the cis male conservative traffic at the end of the day."

"Let's get back to the murdering," Sid says. He catches the micro expression of fear in Jamie's eyes and realizes his phrasing implied something he didn't intend, but he just goes on ignoring that. "Why does somebody want to kill you?"

"I don't know!"

"I call bullshit," Bruce says. "They always know why. You don't go around being a good little sheep and then the man targets you all out the blue. That don't happen."

"But that's exactly what's happening! All my friends are dead! How do you explain that?"

"The cops say most of those were accidents or suicides."

"The fuck they were! I've seen him! He appeared in my kitchen two nights ago—just walked right through the wall and swung a frying pan at me! There he was! Kill Team One!"

"Why do you think he's Kill Team One?"

"That's what Bubbles called him. Scott Fitch-we called her Bubbles. She was transitioning. Bubbles was into all that New World Order conspiracy stuff. She was the first to suspect what was happening after two of the others died. She said that's what they do when you've become a threat to them. They send Kill Team One and he makes you go away."

Sid laughs at the notion. Even when he did do stuff like that, he hardly had time to erase every little bird the powers-that-be deemed an annoyance.

"I figured it was just her coping mechanism. You know? Some people just need to see a reason for everything. They say she jumped off her building, but I know the truth. Not Bubbles. She was a rock. She was in street fights with fascists during Occupy. She just finished collecting funds for reassignment. It didn't make sense."

"Did you go to the police?" Mary Sue asks.

"Do you know what happens when an intersectional person walks into a police station and tells them a secret organization inside the government is assassinating members of the LGBTQ community and allies? It's an understatement to say they don't believe you."

"I don't believe you," Bruce says. "So I understand."

"Bruce, that's mean!" Mary Sue says.

"What? This bitch is trifling. If the NWO had a plan to exterminate all the gay commies in the media they'd have offed Rachel Maddow years ago. And we know Kill Team One ain't doing this shit 'cause he's right here!"

"What?" Jamie chokes, looking frantically around the van, as if the murderous spectre somehow appeared on the floor beside them in response to Bruce's assertion. "Where? Where?"

"He's Kill Team One," Mary Sue says. "The real one."

"What?!"

"There's definitely something going on," Sid says, directing his attention to Bruce and ignoring Jamie's flushed reaction to this revelation. "You saw Graveyard operators here with your own eyes."

"Probably here for the same reason we are. They heard a good story and came to check it out. We know Jamie's story ain't true or they'd have killed them when they snatched them up."

"What did they want from you, Jamie?" Sid asks.

"Those creepy guys in the house?" Jamie specifies. "They said they were trying to protect me from, uh, from you."

"Great," Bruce proclaims with vicious sarcasm. "So if they didn't think you were the mysterious fake homo assassin before, they definitely do now."

"So we just started a conflict with Graveyard because of some bad make-believe. That's spectacular."

"Yeah. And now those motherfuckers are gonna come at us with-shit I don't know—they already got a motherfuckin' werewolf. I don't know what you escalate to after that, but I don't want to find out!"

"Excuse me. . ." Jamie says.

"We should probably try to contact them. Maybe we can draw down."

"Excuse me. . ." Jamie repeats.

"You didn't kill any of those operators, did you?"

"Nah. I just gave Fleabag a headache, but he'll be fine in a few days."

"That should help. Maybe Player has some kind of number we can use to reach out."

"Excuse me. . ."

"We can find them on the sat feed if all else fails."

Jamie explodes into red-faced rage. "How do you dickheads explain the evil ghost killer following me?!"

Sid shrugs. "Figment of your imagination."

"Publicity stunt for your website," Bruce suggests as he chomps off more hot dog.

A dark shape fades through the side of the van, taking up residence in the unoccupied passenger's seat right next to Bruce. The thing is a shadow of a man, grey and ragged like a corpse, but still moving like it is alive. It is covered in rotting greenish grey skin that crackles like a broken salt flat. The creature's atrophied face sags like a zombie's. Its eye sockets are impossibly hollow like some ancient skull, but nothing resides inside except darkness beyond darkness.

"What the fuck?" Bruce exclaims through a big bite of hot dog.

"There you are!" the phantom speaks. Its booming voice echoes into the back of the van. Flakes fall from its cheeks as the crackled skin stretches to permit the movement of its mouth. "I'll end this nightmare now."

Lots of things happen over the course of the next second. Bruce rolls out the driver door. Mary Sue screams. Jamie screams louder. All of the screaming is drowned out by the rapid succession of thunderclaps from the muzzle of Sid's FNX pistol, which he slings from the holster and begins blasting into the empty black holes the weird shadow creature has in place of eyes. At this distance bullets are just a formality; the pressurized gas and burning powder ejected from the muzzle is enough to spall vitreous and scramble brains without any help from lead projectiles. All of that goes through the spectre's head. It just doesn't do any damage on the way through. Sid pops off the entire magazine into that rotten grey face and then leans to get a look at the fresh baseball-sized hole the bullets left in the passenger's side dashboard as he thumbs the mag release.

"Bruce Freeman, Agent of Shield," hisses the ghoulish entity as it scans the repertoire of guns and knives spread through the back of the van. "You're a liar and a coward." As he finishes this proclamation Sid puts a KA-BAR blade through his throat. It's like shadow-boxing. There's nothing of substance there to stab. Sid turns the blade with the ease of a well-oiled doorknob to no effect. He looks back at Jamie and Mary Sue with a wild-eyed look of surprise.

"Run!" Sid bellows. The command is unneeded. Both of them are already on their way out the back doors. The spectre lunges to reach for his fleeing target. Sid moves to push him back toward the front of the van, but the creature jumps right through him into the back of the van. It pauses briefly to make a snarling face back at Sid as it reaches for the small rack of handguns inside the van's gun locker. Sid looks on, wholly dumbfounded, as it plucks an HK USP from the rack and bounds from the back of the van to the blacktop behind it. This is very disconcerting.

Twenty meters down the street, flanked by Mary Sue, Jamie flees in a senseless panic, running against the flow of traffic along the right-hand lane of Michigan Ave. There are no moving vehicles in that particular lane since it is used for parallel parking, but oncoming cars do breeze past them on just the other side of the dotted white line to their right. Smarter prey would have run a different direction, using the van's body to block the ghost assassin's line of sight to them, but that also would have put less total distance between them, and when running from a creature that passes through obstacles like they aren't there, total distance is all that matters. It occurs to Sid that Jamie's blind stupidity may be the only reason

Jamie is the last of the bloggers still alive. The others tried to hide. Jamie just bolted.

"Die, monster!" the ghost-killer shouts as it takes aim at Jamie's back with both hands on the big HK pistol. "For the salvation of us all!"

Jamie is gibbering like a lunatic, but Mary Sue has the presence of mind to look back and see the gun pointed at them. "Get down!" she shrieks, shoving into Jamie with her shoulder. They both go sprawling to the next lane of the street just as a compact car zips past them.

*Bam! Bam!* The shadow man opens fire, hitting a parked car farther down the right-hand lane, and then sending another bullet skidding along the blacktop toward Water Tower Place. The ghost-assassin is a terrible shot.

The real Kill Team One is not. Sid raises his FNX and takes aim at the assailant's back. He can't see the HK from where he stands, but he doesn't have to. He squeezes the trigger once, twice, three times, and renders the HK inoperable by shooting through the shadow creature into the pistol's hammer. The ghost-assassin spends a frustrated second investigating the jammed and shredded gun before tossing it aside. He whips around to curse at Sid.

"Nihilism is your cause, Sid Hansen. Revelry at the cost of woe. Suffering is your wake. How many will drown in it? Families? Cities? Nations?" He turns his coal-black orbs away again to focus on his fleeing target. "Not if I can help it." Then the dark creature gently rises up into the air, lifted by some invisible force, and floats away from the van toward its prey.

Bruce peeks around the corner of the van into the rear doors. "You know that guy?" he asks. Sid shakes his head in the negative before pulling his scary skull helmet down over his face. Somehow, this whole scenario just got weirder. From the gun box he snatches an M4 carbine with attached M203 grenade launcher and leaps into the street.

"Get the van out of here," Sid barks back at Bruce as he charges after the floating ghost. Mary Sue pulls Jamie out of the path of a honking car and they run for the sidewalk in front of a Banana Republic store with the monster in hot pursuit. Sid sifts through ideas of how he might kill the damned thing. He has an extensive knowledge base of unusual creatures mostly due to the old man's insistence that he pass an aptly titled Killing Things Test before going on any real world operations as a youth. This is why Sid knows how to kill werewolves, trolls, redcaps, and even totally ridiculous fictional monsters like vampires. The old man intentionally included a lot of made-up beasties in the training as insurance against outlandish possibilities. Even with all of that knowledge at his disposal, Sid has only vague notions about the ethereal entity he is chasing. It seems to be some kind of ghost, and the old man didn't cover ghosts.

# EXT. THE MAGNIFICENT MILE - DAY

Mary Sue Jadefire Sakura Ravencaller never expected to see something like this in her lifetime—not even working with the notorious Kill Team One on whatever strange and unlikely adventures he might have. Lifeforms that can phase through walls are impossible. Sure, there are forces and objects that can move through solid matter; radio waves, gamma rays, tachyons. A living creature simply cannot for a whole bunch of reasons. Because science. But there it is happening right in front of her—so to speak. It's actually behind her.

Mary yanks Jamie Chan by the arm in a mad dash to the sidewalk nearest them, so they can at least be safe from moving cars. The creature floats toward them, hovering gracefully a meter over the pavement at an unhurried pace. The slow speed at which it levitates is perhaps more unnerving than the fact that it can levitate at all. It is in no rush, as though it is completely confident it will catch them soon enough, regardless of the fact that they are gaining distance from it.

"I should expect better from you, Miss Ravencaller," rumbles the ghostly shade as he passes through a parked sedan on the brim of Michigan Avenue. His shins vanish into the car's roof below him as if he were standing knee-deep in some thin liquid. "You are hardly so shallow—" Whatever else he says is cut off by the resounding explosion of the car into a ball of fire that Mary Sue quickly deduces to be the work of Sid and a grenade launcher. The blast is staggering, and the shock wave pushes Jamie to the ground ahead of her.

Mary glances back as she pulls Jamie up from the pavement again. She can't see the apparition in the cloud of burning car parts between them and the kill team, but she has seen enough already to know the creature wasn't stopped by some simple ordnance.

"We have to lose it somehow," Mary Sue says.

"I tried! It always finds me!" Jamie huffs back. Mary Sue is not convinced by this line of reasoning. She saw the thing's face when it climbed into the van with them. It conveyed just the slightest hint of surprise and even proclaimed *there you are*. It was not the expression of some infallible heat-seeking juggernaut. It was more like some kind of confused transient. That may be the best word for it, because whatever it—he—is, he isn't from around here.

She hangs on to Jamie's hand, tugging the panting journalist along as they run past scores of gawkers stopping to ogle the flaming heap of car in their trail. No one pays the pink haired teen and her companion any attention. Most people don't make the connection because they weren't watching the whole debacle unfold from the beginning—and that's fine. They make it to the crosswalk on Chicago Avenue and Mary looks almost involuntarily to verify the traffic light is still red and it is safe to cross, as if that would halt them anyway. She then glances back to see the transient emerging from the column of smoke in front of Banana Republic with the black shadow of the kill team behind him.

Mary picks up the pace as they cross the street, making it to a mostly grassy block that contains only one small structure: a limestone castle with four crenelated corner towers and one much taller and much more intricately decorated central tower. This is the historic Old Chicago Water Tower.

Automatic rifle fire rings out and people on the street begin to scream. Mary cringes as a series of high powered bullets zip over her shoulder and chip away at the limestone ahead of her. Sid already blew up someone's car, and now he's shooting the historic Chicago Water Tower with an assault rifle, all to hurt a being that has already proven itself impervious to physical damage. She doesn't know which monster she's more afraid of right now.

## SID'S POV DOWN RIFLE SIGHT:

Sid has concerns about over-penetration because he's firing a high caliber automatic rifle at an incorporeal target in a crowded city. Fortunately, nothing but that ugly stone building happened to be beyond the monster. That worked out.

## BACK TO SCENE

Mary Sue hustles past the old water tower looking for somewhere she can turn off of Michigan or otherwise lose the transient. So far they've passed no obvious escape route, just a lot of boutique stores that would turn into a dead end if the transient pursues them inside.

"You know the city better than I!" Mary Sue shouts, prompting a strange glance from Jamie. "Where can we find a large public building with lots of exits? A convention center, shopping complex, tourist attraction?" Mary asks.

Jamie is almost breathing too hard to answer. "Heh, uh, heh. . ." Jamie points across the street. "In there!" And then Jamie takes off running through traffic in a mad dash. Mary Sue has no choice but to follow as cars squeak to a stop. An angry man behind the wheel of a BMW holds down his horn as she passes in front of his grill.

"Sorry!" she squeaks, hopping up the curb and past a glass bus stop shelter featuring a prominent ad for Le Zob cologne. "Sumimasen!"

Jamie whips open the left hand glass double door of a building Mary has been too preoccupied to identify and shoves past a woman and a small girl. Mary darts through the doorway in pursuit, but then halts in terror as she gets a look around the inside of the structure and takes inventory of the clientele.

The pink and burgundy colors in her peripheral vision are the first hint to Mary Sue that she has taken a horribly wrong turn. The brownish red carpets base a veritable labyrinth of tasteful woodgrain cabinets and glass display cases with muted pink backings featuring dozens of very humdrum scenes of daily life—all depicted by poseable, 18-inch tall, baby-faced dolls.

"Oh no," Mary gasps. "No. Not here. We can't be in here!"

This place is packed with parents and small children, most of them young girls. To Mary's left, a woman with a kindergarten aged child in tow flips through a thin paperback book from a display table. "Look honey," she says in a fawning tone. "It's Kit Kittredge."

They are in American Girl Place, the flagship retail location for the iconic brand of historically accurate dolls, doll accessories, and tie-in novels.

"We have to leave now!" Mary Sue says. "We can't be here! He'll tear this place to shreds! Everyone will die!" She isn't sure if she means the transient or the kill team, and it doesn't matter. Mary doesn't need the blood of a hundred children on her hands either way. She turns back toward the door, but is met by the visage of floating death they spent the last several minutes running from in blind panic. She turns back toward the innards of the store and a sea of petrified faces. Their attention starts on her because of what she said, but it quickly shifts to the creature that comes floating through the storefront. Silent, unstoppable, appearing like the destroyer aspect of a god, a living personification of death, it is the absolute last thing that should ever be in this place. In the fraction of a second it takes most of those within sight to recognize this thing, the room falls to chaos.

Women pull young girls away screaming and blubbering. The smart ones flee deeper into the store. Those with less wit go for the nearest corner to cower.

"These children will not shield you! Too much is at stake!" the transient roars. "Tell me, Mary Sue, when the desolate winds are all that moves through this hollow shell of a metropolis, when the nuclear fire has scorched the Earth free of everything we once were, and the scarred survivors feast on the young for sustenance, will little girls still play with dolls?"

The question is insane. The timing is insane. The whole situation is insane. Mary Sue takes the only path there is. She runs deeper into the store. Jamie is already doing the same. Looking ahead, the American Girl store appears to be a cavernous place, divided into sections by large shelving units and temporary walls, with many side rooms and alcoves. It's actually a great place for them to get lost in—excluding the obvious downside of an incidental child massacre.

"You can't escape from me, degenerate!" the transient shouts from behind them. Then he's in front of them. It happens in a blink, so fast that Mary glances back to make sure there aren't two of those monsters. Jamie smacks into the transient full throttle and is flung back against the tile, falling next to a display filled with dolls named Jenny, and nearly tripping Mary Sue in the process.

The transient swipes at the Jenny display with his grey and shriveled hand. The case gives way and broken shards scatter to the floor in a shotgun spread. He snaps a jagged triangle from the frame and wields it like a dagger, raising it over his head to bring it down on Jamie. "Die!" he screams.

Mary Sue reaches out for the closest item of appropriate size and heft, a tin Addy Walker lunch box, which she swings mightily at the transient's makeshift weapon. The box smacks against the glass with a loud crack, and the brittle shard splits into smaller chips in the transient's hands.

"You're a very bad man!" Mary Sue shrieks.

# INT. AMERICAN GIRL PLACE - DAY

Sid does not understand dolls. He never had dolls as a child, or any toys for that matter. He had select fire rifles then, and he has a select fire rifle now. He brings the gun up to his shoulder and trains the red dot of the reflex sight on the transient as the creature takes a swing at Mary Sue. She weaves under it like a golden gloves champ. Behind them, Jamie rises from the floor and runs right through the monster, heading for the back of the store.

The transient is quick to shift his attention from Mary Sue back to the pursuit of his target. He pounces like a jungle cat, bounding past two tables of tiny clothes and tackling Jamie next to a cupboard display of Rebecca dolls with a tablet computer that runs a looping interactive video about the character. The transient pounds Jamie in the back of the head with his flaking fists.

"I'll kill you with my bare hands if I have to!" he shouts, punching Jamie again. Mary Sue dashes to help Jamie, blocking Sid's line of fire in the process—not that it makes much difference. His bullets are apparently useless anyway. He still would like to shoot at the thing more. It may have some solid part which can be harmed, or it may not be incorporeal all the time. It may be that shooting through it is actually hurting it to some miniscule degree. The only way to find out is to blast it to hell and back with zillions of bullets. Unfortunately, this isn't the place for that.

# #JUSTICE

When Sid catches up to the others, Mary Sue is doing her best to grapple with the transient. The monster sits atop Jamie, raining punches down while the terrified blogger tries to slap them away without much success. Mary Sue slaps at the creature's neck and body, trying to get some kind of hold so she can pull him off of Jamie, but her hands just go right through him. In Sid's mind, the interesting bit is that the creature seems to be able to be both solid and incorporeal at the same time, punching Jamie, holding Jamie down, but totally intangible to Mary Sue. He saw the same earlier, when the spectre was impervious to bullets, but holding a gun. Sid aims for the spot where one of the creature's knees is contacting the floor and fires a shot down through its thigh into the carpet. That does nothing.

Sid gets a better idea. He lets the rifle hang from its strap and picks an M84 flashbang grenade from the MOLLE webbing on his armor. He plucks the pin with his thumb and counts as he draws his knife with the other hand. 3 . . . 2 . . . 1 . . . He tosses the grenade only a few feet, sending it on a gentle path through the spectre's head. It explodes midway through those empty black eye sockets.

"Yeow! Yeeagh!" the spectre screams. It tumbles backwards, clawing at its face and yelping until it crab walks into a stack of Kaya dolls. This is very interesting. It can't be shot or stabbed, but it can be blinded. This opens up a large tree of possibilities for Sid to explore. He'll need more flashbangs, and he wonders if he can get anything along the same lines but stronger. Maybe he can permanently blind it with a nuclear weapon. He should also consider damaging the creature's hearing. Some kind of sonic area denial weapon might be effective, and the guys the army leaves to guard those things will be a pushover compared to all the trouble of stealing a nuke. Germ warfare also remains completely unexplored. There's a chemical weapons disposal facility only a few states away. . .

"Go!" Sid commands Jamie and Mary Sue, pointing to the rear of the store. He doesn't have to tell them twice. Jamie is up and running at a shocking pace for someone who just played the part of training dummy in a ground-and-pound demonstration. The others are around the corner from the historical girls display and out of sight in seconds.

The spectre crawls out of the stack of doll boxes, his head emerging from the undisturbed cardboard grid in a disoriented bobbing fashion as he struggles to look up at Sid over the amorphous blobs in his vision. "You're standing on the wrong side of history."

"At least I'm standing," Sid says, looking down on the crawling enemy.

The spectre groans as he rises to his feet. "They told me you would have a terrible sense of humor."

"They should have told you about proper skin care. You look like you were tarred and corn-flaked."

"You've already lost. But it doesn't have to be that way. You can still side with me."

"You look like a used sandpaper condom."

"This isn't funny. Help me kill that abomination and destroy their codification mainframe."

"Are elephant tampons a thing? Because I think that might be the best comparison. You know? Like you're all brown and crusty."

"You're insufferable!"

"You look like a flame broiled booger."

"I'll see you again soon, Kill Team." The spectre vanishes in a blink. Sid lurches backward in surprise and scans the store for any sign of the creature. He notes only the terrified faces of little girls huddled in corners and under tables. Even with the transient gone, they're no less frightened. They're afraid of Sid. It takes him a second to recall he's wearing a combat mask that makes him look like a skull-faced demon ninja. He leans closer to the nearest heap of crying women. They cry harder. Excellent. That means the skull mask is effective.

"Police!" comes a call from the front of the store. Sid leans around a toy display to see two uniformed cops with handguns drawn making their way from the entrance toward his position. The Player hassles him a lot about not killing cops. He tosses a flashbang over the partition into the front room with the cops. He can hear them panicking as he leaves through the back door.

# EXT. HOME DEPOT - UTILITY VAN - DAY

Sid climbs into the rickety utility van and throws his helmet down on the floor. He lost the Chicago P.D. by running down the Red Line subway tunnel to State and Grand, where he aggressively traded clothes with a homeless man and boarded a southbound car with his helmet stashed under a ratty flannel shirt. He rode the train to the Roosevelt station and then walked along the expressway to Home Depot, where Bruce and the others were already waiting with the van on the store's rooftop parking lot.

"Somebody fucked up," Sid says, pulling off the hobo's foul smelling jacket and tossing it out the open van doors onto the ground behind them.

"What do you mean?" Mary Sue says, pressing an ice pack against Jamie's battered forehead as they sit side-by-side in the back of the van.

"That thing had to have followed us from the Graveyard safe house."

Mary Sue shakes her head in vehement denial. "I was sure I lost them!"

"You weren't sure enough."

"I'm sorry," Mary Sue whimpers. "I'll try harder next time."

"We took a lot of turns, Sid," Bruce reasons. "No way that guy followed us from South Side all the way to Streeterville on foot. That's got to be five miles."

"Then how did that ghost-thing, whatever it is-"

"The transient," Mary Sue says.

"Huh?"

"The transient. That's what I call it."

Sid doesn't have time to debate the name, even if it is stupid. "There's no other way the transient could have found us, unless he has a spy satellite."

"We have a spy satellite." Mary Sue cocks her head sheepishly as if the comparison is somehow pertinent- as if the fact that they happen to have a spy satellite somehow means anybody else might just as easily have one.

"I got a better theory," Bruce says. He glares disapprovingly at Jamie Chan. "I think the he-she knows more than we been told."

"You think it gave away our position?"

"They!" Mary Sue says. "You're supposed to say they!"

"That shit's too confusing!" Bruce snorts. "I'm gonna say it! And I think it knows what it wants!"

That isn't any less confusing. "Wait," Sid interjects. "Which it? The he-she it, or the monster it?"

"Motherfucker." Bruce rolls his eyes. "This soy boy motherfucker right here knows what the monster thing wants!"

"I do not!" Jamie insists.

"Probably made a phone call or some shit and gave away the position at least."

Sid snaps his attention straight through Jamie like a bullet. "You have a cell phone?" he snarls. He's tired of warning people about cell phones. The fucking things are practically just tracking devices to anyone with the proper equipment and know-how.

"No." Jamie raises both hands to signify their emptiness, but that obviously means nothing definitive.

"Strip," Sid commands. It looks like he's going to see what Jamie really is after all.

"Nah," Bruce cranks, already averting his eyes. "Just wand the little bitch." Bruce always keeps an RF signal sweeper between the cushions of the van's front seat. He picks it up and holds it out for Sid to take. The sweeper looks like a foot long black plastic wand with a row of light-up LED indicators along the side. Sid takes the wand and begins sweeping and patting Jamie's body despite the journalist's annoyed objections. "How about you tell us more about BuzzWorthy? Who did you people piss off for a scoop? What did you steal? Documents from Groom Lake? You blow the lid off some secret super weapon?"

"We didn't do anything like that!"

"Well you got a motherfucking X-Men-phase-through-walls-motherfucker on your ass. That ain't exactly normal, Kim Jong!"

"Nothing here," Sid declares, finishing his bug sweep.

"I told you," Jamie squeals. "He just finds me wherever I go."

"That don't make sense. Sweeper would have picked up a tracking device, wires, cell phones, any of that."

"He can walk through walls!" Jamie shouts. "Is it so far-fetched that he just knows where I am somehow?"

"Not at all," Mary Sue says. "He could be following some kind of trail, an isotope, a smell, pheromones. It's actually a lot easier to explain than phasing through solid matter. That's completely impossible."

"Welcome to my world," Sid grumbles.

"Hmmm, this is different," Mary Sue says. "The science of intangibility is just, well, junk science. It isn't possible. Even if you find a way to ignore electromagnetism and strong interactions to move through what we perceive as solid matter without damaging any of the particles, that opens up a lot of other considerations."

"You saw him do it," Sid counters. He can't stand when people remain in denial about the ridiculous garbage he deals with on a regular basis, even when it's right in front of their eyes. "Obviously it's not impossible."

"I know! And that's why it won't stop bothering me!"

"I don't get what's such a big deal. He used some kind of super science and made himself walk through walls. Whatever. A guy in a wheelchair once turned into a thirty foot tall dragon and tried to eat me. That was a lot more fucked up."

"But if he's completely intangible, why doesn't he fall through the ground? Like, all the way to the center of the Earth?"

Sid shrugs. "Maybe gravity doesn't affect him either."

"No, silly. The Earth revolves around the sun at a speed a little over eighteen miles per second. Anything that isn't anchored to the planet by gravity gets left behind at an incomprehensible speed. In effect, you would be shot into space instantly."

"But he can fly. We all saw him do that. So maybe he just flies along with us all the time."

"That would be like piloting a drone to keep a laser pointer aimed at a honeybee from exactly a predefined number of micrometers away. It's not technically impossible, I guess. It's just more difficult than the most difficult thing any human has ever done, by several orders of magnitude."

"He ain't all the way intangible then," Bruce says. "His feet are still solid so they're holding him up." It's the simplest explanation, and one that Sid already explored by way of violence.

"I already thought of that." Sid shakes his head. "He gives zero fucks if you shoot him where he should be supported."

"Exactly!" Mary Sue squeaks excitedly. "And even if that were true it would cause even more problems. If only parts of your body are intangible then, in effect, they're cut off. If just your arm phases out, what happens to all that blood flow? Where does it go?"

"It would fly out your shoulder."

"Precisely."

"What about hot dogs?" Bruce asks.

"Huh?" Both Mary Sue and Jamie look peculiarly to Bruce, eyeballing him for a better explanation.

"I mean if he eats a hot dog, then he phases, does that shit just fall out? Or does it phase with him?"

"Not likely. Not unless whatever process made him that way was also applied to the hot dog. It seems like a reasonable assumption that he would discard his entire colon contents too."

"Yummy," Sid interjects.

"That's only the tip of the iceberg. What about lungs that can't interact with oxygen? Neurons potentially firing into nothing? He should be blind because light isn't reflected off his retinas and deaf because percussion doesn't affect his eardrums."

"But we know none of that stuff is accurate. And we've even seen him pick up things."

"I saw him punch through glass," Mary Sue says.

"I saw him punch me in the face a whole bunch," Jamie says, lowering the ice pack to give the others a very nonplussed glare.

"Right. And the whole time he was punching Jamie in the face you were shooting him, so we know for sure he can interact with one object while ignoring another, even though we just established that flies in the face of every natural law."

"Alright." Sid is getting fed up with this. "If he's not an intangible man, then what the hell is he?"

Mary Sue's glossy pink lips form a wavy frown. "I don't know. He could be something really weird. He could be from another universe where electrons and protons are both negative and the laws of physics are all wrong."

"No. He didn't just drift into this reality and start a rampage because of a website. This is personal," Sid says. "He called Jamie a monster. He was angry. He knew my name."

"Mine too," Mary Sue adds. "He asked me if I think little girls will still play with dolls at the end of the world."

"What's a codification mainframe?" Sid asks. He directed the question at Mary Sue, but it quickly becomes evident from her crinkled nose that she does not have an answer. "Jamie?"

"I don't know." Jamie appears as clueless as the rest of them. "Where did you hear it?"

"In the doll store. The transient told me he wants to kill you and destroy the codification mainframe."

"He could mean Narratr."

"The narrator?"

"Narratr, with no O. It's the supercomputer BuzzWorthy is using for a new project."

"BuzzWorthy has a supercomputer?" Mary Sue questions. "I don't want to be rude, but I think you probably mean a server."

"No. I mean a supercomputer. That's what Izzy and Bubbles called it."

"Show me," Sid growls.

# INT. UNKNOWN BUILDING - DUSK

Sid keeps one hand on his gun as Jamie fiddles with a set of keys on a wide ring ahead of him. On the drive over he kept checking the rearview and windows, scanning over passing license plates and committing them to memory in case they appear again soon. He doesn't see any of those plates now, and the narrow lot behind the decrepit warehouse Jamie led them to appears devoid of vehicles, people, and even external lighting.

"It ain't the Waldorf," Bruce says, looking up at the building from behind them. "That's for sure."

It's undoubtedly a real dump of a building; one big block of red bricks and boarded up windows. It is not a great place to be holed up right now because of the lack of easy escape options and an enemy that can walk right through the brick walls. Sid will have to do something about that if they end up here for any extended amount of time.

Jamie gets the door open after what seems like an eternity of key jiggling and lock cranking, then stands and waits for Sid to go on ahead. Sid stands his ground. He isn't interested in walking into a trap. He got a little lazy in that regard during the Red Scare debacle and it cost him. More to that point, he hasn't exactly been ultra-careful with the jihadists, molesters, and gunrunners he has been roasting lately either. This is a good time to cut that shit out, especially with Graveyard in the mix.

Jamie walks on into the darkened warehouse with no extra convincing and only a very brief look of indifference. Sid follows and Mary Sue drags behind cautiously. Bruce remains in the doorway. None of them see as well as Sid in the dark, so he is less uneasy. The group's tension is relieved when Jamie locates what very well may be the only light switch, and the warehouse is illuminated by a dozen racks of bright white LED bars that hang from the ceiling.

There are no ninjas or Soviet assassins waiting for them in the warehouse. There are only dozens of refrigerator sized black computer cabinets lining the walls of the single vast room and arranged into two rows ten meters long through the center of the floor space. The air is thick with the heat of these machines, though they emit none of the whirring noise that Sid would expect from so many computers.

"This is it," Jamie says.

"BuzzWorthy really has a supercomputer." Mary Sue chirps in astonishment.

Sid cannot assign any special significance to anything he sees here. He remains focused on Mary Sue as she inventories the contents of the room. He can almost hear her counting it all up in her head. "Does this tell us anything interesting?" he says.

"Sid, these machines cost over a million dollars per rack and there are sixty-four of them here. An installation like this costs more than BuzzWorthy's estimated net worth." She turns her attention to Jamie. "Where did all this come from?"

Jamie shrugs in embarrassed ignorance. "I thought Izzy bought it."

"Motherfucker," Bruce says. He looks like he wants to tear Jamie's head off. "You think she walked into Best Buy and got same day delivery on this shit?"

"I'm just a journalist. It's not my job to ask questions."

"It is absolutely your motherfuckin' job to ask motherfuckin' questions!"

"What does it do?" Sid demands over the bickering.

"It monitors news sites and social media feeds from sites like Facebook and Twitter."

"How many of them?" Mary Sue sheepishly asks, a look of apprehension creeping onto her face as if she already knows the answer and it disturbs her greatly.

"Uh," Jamie stammers. "I . . . all of them . . . I guess."

Bruce breathes an angry groan. "You guys built your very own private XKeyscore and you're storing it in a shitty warehouse?"

Jamie looks momentarily confused. "What's XKeyscore?"

"It's the shady NSA computer program that steals all the internet data from everybody. How do you not know that?"

"Look, I didn't have anything to do with setting up the machines. I'm not a computer programmer. I'm not an NSA spy. I have a BA in English and a certificate in Postmodern Literature. I couldn't build a latrine much less put together all of this."

"Why do you want to record data which is already publicly available?" Mary Sue asks. She finds a battered little desk near the door, topped by two monitors and a keyboard whose lit indicators imply it is wired to the machine surrounding them. "Is it building some kind of archive?" She taps the ctrl key and both monitors light up.

"I get it," Bruce says. "These shifty motherfuckers got everybody's data and they figure they can auction it off to the highest bidder."

"No!" Jamie insists. "That's not what we're doing!"

"You're tryin' to make the pop-up ads work even better so y'all motherfuckers can cash in."

"Pop-up ads? We don't have pop-up ads! It's not 1998 anymore."

Mary Sue, already typing away at a black screen which is rapidly being populated by little blue alphanumeric characters, endorses that statement. "I don't know, Bruce. Public data isn't very valuable, and you don't need this kind of horsepower to read some browser cookies." She leans in and scans down a long list of blue file headers. Sid can't make any sense of that computer gibberish.

"What about Hillary's emails?" Bruce asks. "You got Hillary's emails on this thing?"

"No! We don't have Hillary's emails! That's not what it does!"

"Then enlighten me," Bruce snarks. "What does it do?"

Jamie hums for a second, uncertain what to say. "I don't know where to start exactly. What do you know about simulated reality?"

Bruce nods. "It's like *The Matrix*."

"No. That's virtual reality."

"Same thing."

"*Not* the same thing."

"Where do I jack in? Does it have the woman in the red dress? I'd like to bend her spoon if you know what I mean."

"It's not a matrix. I wish it was because it would be so much easier to explain. Have you ever heard of Stella Liebeck?"

"No."

"You have. You just don't know her by name. In 1994, a judge awarded her two-and-a-half million dollars because she spilled hot McDonald's coffee on herself."

"That nasty bitch? Yeah, I remember that."

"Do you?"

"Yeah. Bitch had butterfingers when the drive-thru clown handed her the coffee. She spilled it in her lap and took a soccer dive and went after a deep pocket. Everybody knows that story."

"Exactly. Everybody knows *that* story. They don't know the version where Stella Liebeck had horrible third degree burns because McDonalds kept their coffee too hot and she only sued McDonald's for the cost of her medical bills."

"Because that's not what happened."

"Are you sure? What about Michael Brown? Do you know that name?"

"Yeah. He's the dumb thug got shot fighting the police and started the Ferguson riots."

"Not everyone sees it that way. Plenty of people believe Michael Brown was murdered in cold blood. "

"It was a lie. He tried to kill that cop. Went for his gun. Everybody knows that shit."

"Do they? Hands up, don't shoot, right? They still put it on t-shirts."

"Cause people don't read. They're stupid."

"The truth is what people choose to believe. There's a wealth of evidence. Gell-Mann Amnesia, the Mandela Effect, everything Boudrillard ever wrote, the NES Classic hysteria. As long as information is convenient to their worldview, people tend to accept it without verification. If a black teenager gets busted spray painting cars and he doesn't want his parents to think he's a criminal, he might say the cops are out to get black kids. The parents believe it because it fits the mold of the little boy they know. It fits neatly in their worldview. They spread the story. Other people believe it because it conveniently fits their worldview as well. Eventually even some of the cops start to believe it. At that point we're living in a world where the police are out to get black kids just because someone said so. Fact born from fiction. That's hyperreality. It's a simulacrum. It's a perfect model of a real unicorn. It's the most photographed barn in America. It's an illusion made real by nothing but words and repetition."

"Fuck that. The cops do hate black kids. Nobody just made that up."

"You just said they made it up about Michael Brown."

"They made it up about Michael Brown, but not *other* black kids."

"How do you know? Were you there? Did you personally witness every injustice carried out on a black teenager?"

"Now you're just being a pedantic asshole."

"I do believe the police harbor racist attitudes toward dark skinned people, but I can't substantiate it any more than you can. I can't read the minds of every police officer. I can't listen to every discussion they ever had to check for the n word. I don't have slow motion replays of every police involved shooting. I don't have the time in my life to go over every last detail and possible inconsistency of everything I hear. Most of what I know, I know because I was told, and it just felt right somehow. Most of what I know is probably just one of many versions of the truth. Some of it is simply wrong, but from where I stand it's still the truth."

"What are you getting at with this bullshit?"

"Objective truth is a lie. What you call truth I call a narrative—one of many. It's the story you choose to believe. The narrative is reality. It's more real than fact, because it supersedes fact. Change the narrative and you change reality. That's what the machine is for."

"Do you understand any of this?" Bruce says with a bewildered look to Sid.

Sid shakes his head to signal no—fuck no. "I'm only here for the whore money," he says. "Just tell me who to kill."

"I understand it," Mary Sue says. "The machine isn't collecting data. It's analyzing it. It's a crawler."

"Exactly. See, you and I can't listen to every living person's opinion or worldview, but a supercomputer can. It can read every Facebook post, every line of every flame war on the SomethingAwful forums, every piece of CP uploaded to 4chan. The machine knows if you liked *50 Shades of Grey*, agree with Richard Spencer, or think Harvey Weinstein got a bad rap, and it knows exactly how many people think like you and to what degree. It's kind of like the ultimate opinion poll."

"The code is massively expansive and incredibly complex," Mary Sue says as she clicks through pages of code. "I don't think one programmer could have written it all, but I also don't think there could be more than one or two programmers in the world smart enough to understand it."

"So you have a 'roided up Survey Monkey?" Bruce demands, sounding more agitated than before. "I still don't get the point."

"Assuming it works, it maps the collective narrative—what everybody, or almost everybody, believes. The collective narrative is the closest thing there is to objective reality. If I say this is a chair, and Rihanna is a good singer, to us one of those claims is objective fact and the other is a subjective opinion. Even though we know somehow that Rihanna is a good singer, we can't call it a fact. That's only because we don't have the mental capacity to quantify all of the minute qualities that make Rihanna a good singer to millions of individuals. A supercomputer has that capacity. In theory, the machine can objectively state Rihanna is a good singer and why. In theory, it can also identify someone else with those same necessary qualities."

"If you know exactly what made Michael Jackson great, you can just do all those same things and be as great as Michael Jackson."

"In theory, yeah. More or less."

Mary Sue's jaw drops. "A company like BuzzWorthy could write clickbait they know everybody will click."

"That was what Izzy wanted—clicks. She never saw the big picture."

"And the big picture is?"

"The machine could possibly be used to steer shifts in the collective narrative."

"Steer it how?"

"For example, if I want to bring back JNCO jeans, I could tell the machine that, and the machine will pinpoint exactly where in the media sphere to send a message that will bring back JNCO jeans. It might instruct me to get X-celebrity to endorse JNCOs or just write a think piece about them on a blog."

"And you weren't planning to restart the rollerblade craze, were you?"

"I think you can guess the answer to that question."

"You're talking about fake news. You can make fake news you already know everybody will believe."

"We want to promote narratives that are friendly to progress."

"But they're not true."

"If everyone believes it, it's better than the truth. That's the whole point of what I'm saying here."

"That's a real dirty way of thinking."

"Think about the good we might do. We could break down old social constructs and promote equality for everyone. We could train everyone never to cat-call or discriminate based on race or gender. We could make guns and violence so uncool that no one would go near them anymore. The machine might be able to tell us when and where to whisper to start world peace."

"Or where to shout fire in a crowded theater," Bruce winces. "Sid, this thing is a fuckin' doomsday device. We need to destroy it."

"That's a bit of an overreaction. Don't you think? We don't even know if it works yet. It probably doesn't."

"Actually. . ." Mary Sue corrects. "There were queries to the system as recently as this morning. They all came from the same IP." Sid leans over Mary's shoulder to take note of the eight digit IP addresses and timestamps on her screen. "These are going back months. They're all pretty silly." She snorts as she reads off some of the earliest queries. "Dollhouse was better than Firefly. Crocs make you jump higher. A blood diamond means more than other diamonds because someone died for it. Cigarette smoking can prevent Alzheimer's. Eating a marble every day cleanses toxins from your body. Pegging is what your man secretly desires. Puffy shirts are manly in a non-ironic way. Flu shots cause erectile dysfunction."

"Does this stuff make sense to you?" Sid asks. It all sounds like nonsense to him.

"No," Jamie says. "That stuff isn't true."

"The truth is a lie," Bruce mocks. "There's no such thing as the truth."

"I don't understand. Why would somebody enter this nonsense? "

"It could be a trial run," Mary Sue theorizes. "Whoever put in the queries recorded the results, did what the machine recommended, and now they're waiting to see if cigarette sales increase."

"But why?" Jamie still looks stunned. "Why didn't they say anything?"

"Dammit, bitch! Do you need the spy hunter to spell it out for you? You all got played! Set up! You were just patsies!"

"For who?"

"The fucker who built the damn thing. We still don't even know who that is."

"That doesn't make sense. What for?"

"This." Bruce points at the computer. "This thing is a motherfucking shitstorm! The mystery man knows that. And he also knew if it ever got built, a whole bunch of awful would come his way in the form of ghost assassin motherfuckers and who-knows-what-else awful shit. So he set you all up for that. He made it look like you kids built this thing on your own so you would take the heat. Then you all end up dead, or not, maybe he doesn't even give a fuck. Either way he walks away with what he wants."

"What do you think he wants?"

"Dunno, but safe bet it's not to make the Macarena huge again."

After all this, they still don't have anything close to an explanation to the most important question of the day. "Why does the transient want to kill whoever built the machine?" Sid asks.

"Fuck if I know," Bruce says. "Ask him next time you see him. You got Semtex in the van right? Let's wire it up. Whoever this motherfucker is, we're gonna take his toy away."

"Semtex is largely concussive," Mary Sue argues. "Even if you bring down the whole building it won't damage the platters enough to prevent data recovery. It would be better to burn the drives."

"Thermite? I get to make thermite?" Sid says, practically drooling at the prospect. He doesn't have an excuse to mix up incendiaries nearly often enough.

"I think gasoline will do just as well."

Sid's spirits are instantaneously deflated.

"You guys can't be serious," Jamie whines. "This machine could be a way to real attainable social justice. Not some Marxist college kid fantasy, but the real thing."

"Aight. I'm gonna take the van out and fill up some gas cans," Bruce says, jingling his keys on the way out the door.

"Let me get my laptop before you go." Mary hops up from the computer terminal to follow him.

"Bring me the smelting stuff and the Murder Machetes," Sid shouts after her.

"They're not Murder Machetes!" Mary Sue squeals back at him as she vanishes through the doors, leaving Sid and Jamie alone in the warm cavern of blinking LEDs and boxes.

"This is a huge mistake," Jamie says. "You can't listen to them. You really think destroying this machine will keep whoever built it from just making another one? Or somebody else? As long as it's possible somebody will eventually do it. What if it's Nazis? Or just some corporation that wants to sell cola? We can't have people like that controlling the narrative. We have to get ahead of them and we have that chance right now, maybe never again."

"I don't understand much of this," Sid says. "But the people who grabbed you earlier, the New World

Order, they seem to think this supercomputer you guys built is going to cause some kind of apocalypse."

"So you just believe them?"

"No. They lie all the time. They're a secret shadow government. That's what they do best. I just figure I'm here; so is the postmodern doomsday computer. Might as well scrap it. What can it hurt?"

"Everything. You know there are some people who actually need change. We can't keep living with the way things are. You know almost half of transgender people attempt suicide?"

"Pussies."

"You don't know how hard it is. When I was nine, the school made me use the nurse's bathroom because the boys and the girls didn't want me in theirs. They called me she-male."

"When I was nine, I spent the winter in the woods fashioning stone daggers to kill deer for meat and pelts," Sid says. "Sometimes I slept inside the warm carcasses."

"Okay, yeah, that's not really a fair comparison." Jamie exhales aggravated air. "It doesn't mean people like me don't have a right to exist."

"Nobody has rights to anything. All that matters is what you can kill and what you can't."

"You can't believe that."

"Why not?"

"That's like pure nihilism! Nobody actually believes that. It flies in the face of social contract theory. Nobody lives that way."

Sid shrugs. "I do."

Mary Sue returns hauling a laptop case, along with the bag of stuff Sid picked up at the Home Depot and a nylon belt attached to two sheathed matte black KA-BAR machetes which she drops on the floor next to him.

"And when somebody just comes and takes whatever they want from you, you'll be okay with that?" Jamie posits.

"I'll kill them," Sid says.

"What if they have guns?"

"I'll kill them."

"What if it's the government?"

"I'll kill them."

"You know Sid is a genetically engineered super soldier, right?" Mary Sue says. Sid shifts his gaze her direction and observes her to be in an unintentionally suggestive position as she crawls on all fours under the desk where the computer terminal is situated. Her tiny denim shorts hardly contain the luscious booty pointed at him like a cannon. "He solves all of his problems by killing someone."

"I'm not genetically engineered," Sid says, briefly mesmerized by dat ass. He wrests his attention back to Jamie for some intimation that the journalist might also be ogling, but only finds Jamie glaring at him in quiet judgment. Noteworthy. Jamie isn't interested in the booty.

"You're quicker than any unaugmented human, and stronger than most professional bodybuilders. Your jaw was broken in three places just last month and you already show no sign of discomfort." Mary Sue scoots backwards from under the desk, having connected whatever cables she needed. "Also, bullets never hit you."

"That shit again? I told you, I'm just good at utilizing cover."

"I don't know, Sid. The data doesn't support that. Who was your mother?"

"I have no idea."

"Your father never talked about her?"

"No. It doesn't mean they grew me in a tube. You have pink hair. Does that mean somebody grew you in a tube?"

"Don't be silly. I'm part Fae."

"Huh?" Jamie says, dumbfounded.

"Yeah, what?" Sid echoes.

"I'm part Fae on my mom's side," Mary Sue answers, as if that should clear everything up without further explanation. "I wish I wasn't. I'm a stupid ugly freak."

Jamie speaks up before Sid can say anything. "You look like a Michael Turner drawing brought to life with magic."

"Thanks, Jamie," Mary says. "But you don't have to lie to make me feel better. I came to terms with the way I look."

"It's not a lie. You're a major babe," Sid says.

"That's really cruel, Sid," Mary pouts. "I don't patronize you by saying your voice isn't creepy."

"Oh, I'm glad it's not just me then," Jamie breathes a sigh of relief. "He sounds like angry Jack Bauer all the time, doesn't he?"

"I'm not patronizing you," Sid sneers. "Every inch of you is weirdly perfect, except for that stupid little microscopic scar you always whine about. How did you get that thing anyway?"

"I don't want to talk about it."

"Did you get nicked by a monomolecular razor? What's that small?"

Mary Sue purses her lips quietly, then abruptly changes the subject. "I'm going to save all the queries on my laptop in case we need them later."

"Alright. I got shit to do too," Sid says. "Jamie, you just sit here and try not to die." Jamie compliantly sits down on the floor next to Mary Sue and her laptop as Sid hauls the shopping bags from Tiffany's and Home Depot to the other side of the warehouse.

Sid spends the next twenty minutes turning the Murder Machetes into werewolf slaying swords of killy kill death. He couldn't find a crucible at Home Depot. The store clerk didn't even seem to know what that was, so he has to make due. Not a problem. Sid hangs one of the silver Tiffany's bracelets around the blade of a machete and holds the 18-inch blade out in front of him as he heats the silver with the butane torch. The bracelet slowly gains an orange glow, then softens and begins to melt onto the KA-BAR. He turns the blade carefully, allowing the silver to spread against the flat of the blade on both sides near the razor pointed tip. This works because silver melts at a much lower temperature than the 1085 carbon steel KA-BAR uses to forge knives. The final product is an uneven coating of splotchy silver that coats only some of the blade in an uneven ring. It isn't pretty, but Sid is confident it will put a permanent perforation in that werewolf. He grafts another bracelet to the other machete and then leaves both weapons to cool on the floor before he walks back across the warehouse to where Mary Sue is once again situated in a compromising position. Her face is buried in the laptop screen on the floor in front of her. The keyboard could just as easily be a viciously abused pillow in another setting.

Jamie is sitting on the floor behind her, and this time Jamie is most definitely ogling the booty.

Sid stands silently, also taking in the view for a moment before he says anything. "Take a picture," he finally says, his sudden presence causing Jamie to flinch and whip around to expose reddening cheeks. "It'll last longer."

"A picture of what?" Mary Sue asks, looking back at them obliviously. She blinks several times, quietly waiting for an answer that never comes.

"Nothing." Sid grins at Jamie derisively. "Anyone have a pen?"

Mary Sue nods and fishes a pen from her laptop case. Sid uses it to write a complex chemical formula on the back of a Home Depot receipt: $C_{11}H_{26}NO_2PS$

"I need you to make this for me," Sid says. He hands the slip of paper to Mary Sue and she reads the formula. Her nose crinkles with distress.

"Sid," she squeaks. "This is the formula for VX nerve agent!"

"Yeah."

"I can't make this for you! I won't!"

"Why not?"

"This is a chemical weapon of mass destruction! A soda can of it could kill everyone in Chicago!"

"You want to make nerve gas?" Jamie joins in the argument. "That's a violation of international conventions, and federal law, and human decency."

"You guys are blowing this out of proportion." Sid rolls his eyes. "I used to smear Revenant TXX on my knife and stab people with it."

"What is that?" Jamie asks.

"It's another nerve agent," Mary Sue answers. "Highly classified. It's considered deadlier than VX."

"Yeah," Sid says. "Messier too."

"Well, I won't make you VX. That's out of the question."

"What about Sarin? That's like VX for kids."

"It is not! Biowarfare agents are not for children! These things are extremely hazardous! You need a chemwar suit just to handle them."

"Meh. You tape some trash bags together. It's really not a big deal. I've done this before."

"I'm not making you any nerve agents."

"Okay. I guess Jamie can just die then." Sid lifts his shoulders in a sarcastic dismissal of Jamie's plight. "Sorry, Jamie. Mary Sue is too much of a goodie good to save your life."

"Sid! That's not fair!" Mary Sue cries out. "You don't even know if VX will affect him."

"Do you have any better ideas?"

"Sonic weapons are a possibility. First we need to see how he reacts to loud noises."

"You want to crank up Dethklok and see if that puts him down? Great plan."

"It's a working hypothesis. That flashbang grenade seemed to irritate him."

"Where's Bruce? Shouldn't he be back by now?"

"Player called while you were smelting swords over there. Bruce is taking a longer route. Something about avoiding cameras."

"If we're gonna be here for a while, maybe we should order some pizzas or something." Pizza delivery is a new fascination for the kill team. He has ordered a number of pizzas in the last few weeks, all from random landline phones near the firehouse, and directed to a variety of other addresses within several blocks. He wouldn't want to establish a pattern for anyone watching and planning to poison him.

Jamie only glares bitterly at Sid.

"I like pizza," Mary Sue says. "What kind of pizza?"

## INT. UTILITY VAN - NIGHT

The quest for gasoline is not an easy one. In a city like Chicago, there are cameras everywhere. Most of the gas stations have them inside and outside, and many of the intersections have them mounted on utility poles. This means some record of Bruce purchasing gas will exist no matter what precautions he takes. He won't be able to stay completely anonymous, but there are ways to mitigate his risks.

He starts by driving out into the suburbs. He wants to be pretty far from the scene of the crime. Local police and fire investigators will most easily obtain information from sources within their jurisdiction. Outside of that they have to take extra steps. Bruce wants to make sure extra steps turn into extra extra extra steps—more than most authorities will bother to take investigating a warehouse fire in which no one was hurt.

He puts on a doo rag, sunglasses, and fake lumberjack beard before stepping out of the van in front of the Walmart in Orland Park. He doesn't want to leave any recognizable images of himself on the store security cams. He isn't so worried about the van. It is registered to an outlaw biker he and Sid buried in West Texas not long ago. Maybe next week it will be registered to some other body.

Inside the supermarket, Bruce takes a quick jaunt back to the automotive department and loads a shopping cart with five-gallon gas canisters. He pays cash at the self-scan checkout. He is whistling *Uptown Girl* the whole time.

Next, he travels east to a Mobil station nearby. He doesn't even get funny eyes from the clerk as he purchases a bottle of Mountain Dew Pitch Black, two Black & Mild filter tips, and forty dollars' worth of prepay on pump number three. He fills three and a quarter cans on the forty bucks, then heads out looking for the next gas station. He wants to go to multiple stations to keep moving and avoid eyes. A guy with a fake beard spending an hour on one pump to fill up a dozen gas cans is suspicious. Somebody might notice that and ask questions.

In the rumbling van, the Player speaks from Bruce's cell phone propped up in the console cup holder. "I only have a week's worth of surveillance stored, but there's no activity on the feed until you guys walked in there."

"It was a long shot anyway," Bruce says. "I doubt homeboy would be dumb enough to go near the hardware after he went through all the trouble to set up BuzzWorthy. Just keep your eyes peeled for lookie loos."

"I'm all over it. Those Graveyard goons are on the other side of the city."

"I'm not worried about Graveyard. The damn transient hopped right in the van to say hi."

"He materialized next to you. I saw it on the feed."

"Got any theories yet there?"

"None. I've never seen anything like it."

"The sooner we toast this fucking computer and get out of town, the better."

# INT. UNKNOWN BUILDING - NIGHT

"So do I call you he or she?" Sid says. He bites the end from a rubbery pizza crust as he glares at Jamie over the open pizza box on the floor between them.

"Neither. You're supposed to say they."

"But you have to be one or the other."

"You're so hung up on this," Jamie says. Mary Sue frowns uncomfortably.

"Because it's really fucking weird. I can tell you're faking whatever you are, but I can't tell if you're a man badly imitating a woman, or a woman badly imitating a man."

"What hurts me most about it is that of all the freaky stuff that happened today, this is the thing that stuck out to you."

"That makes me think you're a chick, because only a chick would whine about some feelings bullshit like that, but maybe you know that and that's part of the act."

"It's not an act. I'm non-binary. I'm neither male or female. You don't have to be one or the other."

"You have a penis *and* a vagina."

"No."

"Then there's nothing down there? It's just flat?"

"No. Sid, gender is more than just what body parts you have. There are lots of genders, and not everybody identifies with the gender that doctors assigned them at birth."

"I don't think doctors put penises and vaginas on babies."

"That's not what I meant."

"Then how does that last thing you said make sense?"

"Because sometimes, some people don't feel like they're the gender everyone else says they are. Most people are born and told that they're a boy or a girl, and they're fine with that. Those people are called cisgender."

"I'm cisgender," Mary Sue says.

"Yes you are," Jamie says. "You really, really are. The thing is some people aren't comfortable with being the gender they were told they are. They feel like they're the opposite gender, or maybe something in between. Maybe someone who was thought to be a girl isn't a girl at all. Maybe she's still mostly a girl, but she likes big trucks and hates miniskirts and high-heels."

"Lesbians."

"No—well, yes. Sometimes they're also lesbians. Lesbians are people who identify as female and are also attracted to people who identify as female. But a lesbian could have been assigned a male gender at birth."

"So then they're a man pretending to be a lesbian?"

"No, they're transgendered."

"So you have a dick, but you're a lesbian."

"No."

"If I tell chicks I'm a lesbian will more of them want to fuck me?"

"No. That's not how it works. You don't just get to pick."

"It sounds like you did."

"No. I was always this way. Other people told me I was something else, but they were wrong."

"Seriously, though. How much box are you pulling with this scam?"

"I'm not. . ." Jamie makes an exaggerated face of disgust at Sid's turn of phrase. ". . .pulling any box."

"Really? You find guys that are into whatever you are?" Sid makes a rotten face as he involuntarily glances down Jamie's form.

"No. And men can fuck right off."

"Gay guys then? Cause you look like a man. That makes sense, right?"

"Not that it's any of your business, but I've been with a number of trans women, and in college my partner was agender, although she's not that anymore."

"What did she turn into?"

"A Republican, but that's neither here nor there."

"But she's a she?"

"Now, yes. Before that her pronoun was xie."

"What the fuck is that?"

"Some people don't want to be called he or she or they. They want to be called xie, hir or ne, or something else even."

"No. This is fucked. This is worse than when I tried to learn the stock market."

"Is it that hard to believe that there might be more than two genders?"

"Yes. I've seen a lot of people. I've killed a lot of people. All of them were one or the other."

"That's just because they were all socialized that way. Gender is a social construct. It's a narrative like the Michael Brown story or the moon landing. It's just a made up thing that everybody believes. It's not real."

"You said if everyone believes something that makes it true."

"No I didn't."

"You said 'We want to promote narratives that are friendly to progress' and then Bruce said 'But they're not true' and you said 'If everyone believes it, it's better than the truth.'"

"That's not the point!"

"Then you said 'That's the whole point of what I'm saying here.'"

"What are you? A human tape recorder?"

"He remembers everything," Mary Sue says. "I really think they grew him in a tube."

"I'm confused now," Sid says. "Is it not true if everybody believes it?"

"I think I don't want to talk about this anymore." Jamie grumbles. "Is that an HK416 or an M27 IAR?" Jamie asks, pointing at the rifle on the floor beside the pizza box.

"Those are both HK416s. M27 is just the military designation for the variant with the sixteen-point-five inch barrel. This one is two inches shorter. Hold on—you know about guns?"

"Yeah. I was really infatuated with them in high school. It was a rebellion sort of thing."

"You fought in a rebellion?"

"No--like a teenage rebellion. You know."

"No. I don't know."

"You never argued with your parents?"

"You don't argue with the old man, so much as get your ass kicked by the old man."

"At least you had a dad. Mine bailed early. I can't blame him though. My mom is a fucking headcase."

"My dad made me fight grown men in a cage, to the death, in increasing numbers until I could kill ten at a time barehanded."

"My mom wanted me to be a girl so bad she made me wear pink dresses until I was twelve. We had a mandatory Barbie hour every day with both tea and crumpets. She cried and threatened to hang herself when I told her I wasn't doing that anymore."

"What the hell is a crumpet?"

"It's a miniature pancake. That's all it is. They should just call them small pancakes."

"The old man only fed us raw meat, water, rice, and mixed vegetables."

"Mom gave me a bottle until I was six. She made me sit in a car seat until I was fourteen."

"I had to drift a Honda Accord down a spiral parking garage ramp with an angry wolverine chained to the steering wheel when I was nine. The old man called it defensive driving training."

"Mom once called nine-one-one because there were, quote, too many Mexicans on the grill line at Panda Express. They actually sent a car. She was off her meds and freaking out. The police didn't know what to tell her. It was so embarrassing. That was the first time I ran away. I stayed at my friend Pat's house and we shot his grandpa's MG42 all weekend. I never wore that pink dress again."

"A machine gun moment. I've had a few of those."

"I could probably use a few more," Jamie sighs. "So how is that gun different from an M4 or an AR-15?"

"It's short-stroke gas piston operated." Sid points at the HK416. "There's a piston above the barrel that the gases blow back on discharge. The piston strikes the bolt carrier and forces it back."

"Is that better?"

"Yeah. Direct impingement blows fouling back into the bolt carrier assembly and makes jamming more common with the standard AR-15."

"You really know your machine guns."

"It's not a machine gun. It's a select fire rifle."

Mary Sue screams.

"You're way too excited about this," Sid says.

"Behind you!" Mary Sue shrieks. Sid is on his feet in a millisecond.

The transient treads toward them through the open warehouse. The silver smelted KA-BAR machetes are like infantry sabers in the grey creature's molting hands. Rotting and naked yet again; its skin appears even more ragged than before. His hair hangs in stiff white strands that point like arrows at the floor. "This place," he says, dragging the machetes along behind him. The tips screech on the cracked cement. "This is it. The engine of so much emptiness."

"We're going to burn it," Sid says, hopping up from the floor. "But you have to leave Jamie alone. This was all a setup. Jamie doesn't even know how the machine works."

"You can't believe a word that changeling utters. Every sentence is a perfect lie and a perfect truth."

"That really doesn't correspond with what I've seen." Sid sneers. He can hardly imagine Jamie as some sort of evil mastermind—a little kooky for sure, but in no way dangerous.

"It corresponds with deceit and destruction. The machine is only an instrument. It's the musician that must die!" Without another second's hesitation, the transient raises both weapons over his cadaverous head and then swings them down like guillotine blades at Jamie. Sid rips the nearby terminal's monitor from its place, trailing cables and flailing an optical mouse along with it, to intercept the huge knives. The blades sink deep into the LCD display which hisses and crackles. Sid twists the computer peripheral to loosen the transient's grip, then grasps one of the machete handles to wrench it free.

Jamie backs into the corner near the tussled PC terminal at first, then dashes for the door while Sid is tangled with the ghostly creature. Mary Sue throws a small PC speaker through the transient's head to absolutely no effect. The monster pries free the machete it managed to hold on to, then turns and follows Jamie out the door. Sid takes a swing at it and his weapon glides through the creature's back like air as it runs from him. That at least confirms it does not have a silver allergy—though the odds of that were already quite long.

"It doesn't fucking stop," Sid says as he chases the transient through the door. The monster gains on Jamie, but Sid catches up just as quickly. When the transient raises his weapon to strike again, Sid steps through the intangible creature and deflects the machete with his own. The angle could not be any more awkward, or the situation more ludicrous. The transient takes another swing, which Sid parries to his right—both of their rights since they occupy the same space. This is officially the weirdest sword fight of all time.

The transient halts suddenly and nearly jams Sid in the guts with the butt of the machete as he isn't able to stop that fast. Sid leans left and narrowly avoids the blade as he rolls forward on the blacktop lot outside the warehouse. He regains his feet just in time to block the transient's machete again.

"Your interference is beginning to upset me, Kill Team," the transient snarls.

"You want to be upset? Look in a mirror, cocksucker."

"I thought yo-" Whatever the transient was trying to say gets interrupted when Mary Sue blows an air horn in the center of his skull.

*Bwoooooo!* The transient recoils and slaps his hands over his ears as he dives to escape the shrill squealing of the horn. "Gaah!" he croaks, his machete clacking against the blacktop. "What is that horrible thing?"

"I knew it!" Mary Sue says.

The transient lashes out and rips the air horn from her hands. He crushes it between his palms and it bursts into a frosty explosion of compressed air.

Sid scoops up the fallen machete and slides both weapons back into their sheaths on his back. There seems to be no use in swiping at the transient with them. He finds the particulars of this enemy especially frustrating. Sid has never been so strictly on the defensive before. He usually subscribes to the theory of good offense being the best defense, shooting foes dead before they have any ability to act against him, but that doesn't apply here at all. He can distract this thing, maybe annoy it, but he can't hurt it at all. He can only try to prevent it from doing any damage. It's the worst feeling in the world: not being able to kill someone.

Sid turns to see Jamie sprinting full bore down the street with a good lead on all of them. That kid really can move. The transient floats off in pursuit. Again, Sid follows.

The creature moves at a brisk pace when it levitates, but not anything the kill team can't keep up with. Jamie turns off the sidewalk down a narrow alleyway one block from the warehouse, which is a bad move. The transient cuts the corner into the alley by phasing through it, its chief advantage in any foot race. Sid loses sight of the ghostly being for a few seconds as he catches up to the alleyway and also takes the corner. When he regains sight of the other two, Jamie is still running like mad, but the transient has stopped to pick up a brick from the ground beside a heavy steel dumpster. He winds up and launches the brick at Jamie's head from meters away, but Sid bats it out of the air as it leaves the creature's hand. The brick cracks against the alley wall. The transient growls with frustration as he bats at Sid's head with a clenched fist. Sid raises a gauntlet and catches the creature's comparatively feeble punch—for the first time actually contacting the transient in any way resembling normal physical interaction. It is not stronger or faster than any normal human, at least not according to its punching ability. The only unusual note is that the monster does not appear to damage his hand throwing a full force haymaker into a gauntlet made from metal and carbide plates. Sid knocked a werewolf's teeth out with that gauntlet. This scrawny creep should have just broken at least some of the bones in his hand, but he seems fine.

Then, in the microsecond the transient's fist is frozen only inches from his face, Sid notices a peculiar pattern. It is faded and blurry and difficult to make out against the background of grey flesh, but it is definitely there. The transient has a single line of words and numbers tattooed on the underside of his wrist, too small to read or notice from even a few meters away: Aqua 6 1 6 Green.

"Is that your model number?" Sid says, provoking a very morbid glare in return.

The monster sails away in an instant, continuing its single-minded pursuit of Jamie.

Mary Sue catches up to them again just as Sid takes off down the alley. "I don't think he gets tired," she yells.

"Neither do I," Sid snarls back.

"I mean really though. He can even fly. Jamie can only keep running so long."

She does have a point. Sid can sprint for miles, but Jamie will be out of steam soon, and it's Jamie the thing is after. This isn't quite the foot race it appears to be. It's more like running from a slow car.

"You have to find a way to hurt him or he's going to kill Jamie!" Ahead of them, Jamie comes to the end of the alley and turns out of sight. The transient slips into the brickwork beside him to pursue through the nearest building. Sid and Mary Sue increase pace to make up for the monster's ability to shortcut.

"I might know a way, but *somebody* won't make me VX!"

"You can't use nerve agents in the city!" Mary Sue shrieks. "That's horrible!"

"You're being a total bitch about this!"

"I am not a b-word! You're so mean!"

As they come around the corner and regain sight of Jamie, Sid sees that the journalist may have already discovered a way to solve their dilemma—at least for the short term. Jamie has crossed through an empty street and is trundling up a set of tan-painted metal steps to the elevated 'L' train platform above. The free floating stairs are covered by a ribbed tin roof and enclosed with glass.

Sid charges out into the street as the transient wisps over the trunk of a rusted out hooptie parallel parked near the stairway to the train platform. The creature watches Jamie ascend the steps and begins its own gravity defying elevation from the pavement. Sid makes it to the bottom of the stairway in time to see Jamie struggling up the steps in an apparent effort not to pass out from exhaustion. Jamie's cardio fitness is crap.

There is a turn-around landing in the staircase two thirds of the way to the top, and as Jamie reaches it the ghoulish head of the transient phases through the metal flooring ahead. Sid charges up the steps full speed to intercept the monster, but Jamie is too gassed to focus on anything but making it up the steps. Jamie practically runs face-first into the transient without even an attempt to stop. The transient gives one vicious push that shoves Jamie backward down the steps. Luckily, Sid is there to stop the blogger from tumbling all the way down to the bottom and ending up with a broken neck.

"Your presence is quite frustrating Kill Team," the transient grumbles as he punches the window beside him. The glass ripples loudly, but doesn't break. It's probably safety glass. Sid could break it, especially with these nifty dread gauntlets, but the transient failing to do so further cements Sid's speculation that the ghost cannot match his strength. "Haven't you ever dreamed a dream so real and good that waking up felt like a nightmare?"

Sid steadies Jamie on the steps with him and pulls a grenade from the MOLLE strap across his chest. Mary Sue stops at the bottom of the steps behind them, watching apprehensively as Sid yanks the pin.

"All you wanted after was to go back to sleep, back to the dream, but the dream was gone. . ." The transient coughs a throaty hack and reels momentarily. Blood from his mouth spatters the handrail he clutches to support himself. "Don't you understand that this world is my dream? I do this for us all, so that the morning will never come."

"Cock-a-doodle-doo, asshole," Sid says. He throws the grenade up the steps. The little olive canister clanks down on the landing at the transient's feet and he watches with a visible sense of confused fascination as it rolls through his ankle and taps against the glass behind him. It stops with stenciled white lettering face-up reading M18 SMOKE GREEN. That only seems to increase the transient's bewildered state.

"What are you doing?" he says, as the grenade pops and begins pouring forest green smoke into the air. The enclosed stairway fills in seconds.

"I can't see!" Mary Sue shrieks.

Sid drags Jamie forward up the stairs through smoke so thick he can't see past the end of his own nose. They reach the landing, where Sid knows they are actually standing in the transient, and he pushes Jamie up the next short flight of stairs.

"It's clever in a way, I suppose," the transient rasps. "But you've only blinded us both." Sid stomps on the floor as Jamie vanishes up the stairs into the inky green mist. A hand almost instantly clamps down on his armored shoulder. "There you are!"

"Wrong!" Sid shouts as he turns and punches the transient in the mouth. "Whoever told you about me missed some important details." Sid bobs aside of a withered fist aimed right at his chin. "See, the old man taught me to fight. Ninjas taught the old man to fight. Ninjas don't need eyes to see." Sid takes another swing at the transient and feels his gauntlet bash into something meaty, but the next punch after that goes through nothing but air. Curiously, the billowing smoke seems undisturbed by the transient's movements through it.

"You're an obstinate buffoon if you think this path is anything but the wrong one." If Sid hit any normal human that hard with his armored hands they wouldn't be crawling, much less speaking coherent sentences. Punching the transient does nothing. He decides to back off and see to it that Jamie makes it onto the train.

Sid bolts up the stairs and emerges from the green cloud onto the platform flanking the 'L' train tracks at whatever station this is—he didn't bother to check. Jamie is already jumping the turnstile ahead of him and rushing for the open doors of the awaiting train car. Nearby, the transient rises through the platform floor searching both directions for his target. He quickly zeroes on the only frantically fleeing human shape, and both he and Sid give chase.

Jamie steps onto the train car just as Sid leaps over the turnstile. The doors slide closed before he can make it aboard, and a gasping petrified Jamie watches as the transient approaches. The damn thing isn't leaving the station nearly fast enough. Sid whips a machete from his back and jams the point of the blade into the crack between the car doors, drawing unwanted attention from the half dozen bystanders inside the train.

"That guy has a sword!" somebody shouts, but collective attention of the other passengers is quickly stolen by the floating naked cadaver that fizzles through the side of the car.

Sid twists the machete handle to try and pry the doors open as the train begins moving. He gains a certain curiosity about who's running this train, and why they're just going about business as usual even though an armored ninja guy is stabbing through the doors and a ghostly apparition just floated aboard, but on second thought the reaction doesn't seem entirely unjustified. Why not hit the button for get-the-hell-out-of-here?

Sid has no success getting the door open before the train is moving too fast and a passing support beam on the platform threatens to snap his machete from the train, so he pulls the big knife loose and circles the beam. As the train car accelerates on the tracks and passes him, Sid leaps onto the rung-like connectors between it and the next car. He sheathes the machete and draws an FNX, which he uses to blast through the nearest window. Squeezing through the broken glass around the window is relatively easy with a layer of Kydex protecting him.

Sid tumbles onto one of the blue-on-white aisle facing seats inside the car and rises next to a sign citing safe procedures in case of emergency. One of the items on the list reads: Move to another car if your immediate safety is threatened. All of the passengers seem to be following that directive. A small stampede of frightened faces nearly tramples Sid to get away from the death spectre standing at the other end of the car. Sid elbows a large Hispanic man who seems too incompetent to move around him, then has to climb over someone in a wheelchair at the end of the rush, but he manages to clear the wall of bodies as they all pour into the next car, leaving him alone with Jamie, the transient, and a crusty old man who looks around the inside of the car, shakes his head, and returns to sleep on a tattered travel pillow.

"You're getting on my nerves, Sid," the transient says, snatching the handle of an empty baby stroller someone left in the aisle of the car. "You can't fight me." He whips the stroller angrily against the row of seating beside him. "You can't hurt me. You can't hold me back. I never get tired. You can never do anything but run, and you can't run forever, so why prolong the inevitable?"

"Whore money," Sid says. This actually seems to throw the transient off.

"Whore money?" the ghastly thing spits in disbelief, brown blood dripping from his lips.

"Yeah. It's money for whores. It's about all money is really good for."

"I wish I could have as cavalier an attitude. Where I come from, those trivialities are long expired. You have no idea what you have." The transient reaches up to the ceiling between the nearest set of sliding doors, into a darkened well the width of a coffee mug which contains some kind of small handle. "Well, no matter. I'll set it right soon." He pulls the handle and the doors slide open, admitting the cold night wind and rumbling rail sounds to the interior of the car. The second and third stories of buildings roll by in the darkness. "Time to go for a dive."

"Jamie, run," Sid barks, but the transient is too quick. He snatches Jamie's wrist and hauls them both through the open doors.

Sid bounds forward, reaching for Jamie's flailing hands as they go out the doors. He gets nothing but slapping fingertips until he himself is out of the train, hanging onto the door frame with one hand and Jamie's wrist with the other. At the bottom of the human chain they have formed, the transient dangles from Jamie's right foot, screaming with wild elation as he weighs them down like a sack of cinder blocks dragging a loose-lipped mobster to a watery grave. "Die, charlatan! Die!" Only seconds down the line, the front of an oncoming train approaches like a wall of steel death to scrape them all from the side of the car.

Sid roars and strains to curl two adult people back into the train car. As the transient is lifted toward the doors, his demeanor shifts from a victory celebration to pure quivering rage. He underestimated the kill team's strength. The creature vanishes and with its weight gone, Sid yanks Jamie back into the car just as the other train whooshes past them.

The transient is already waiting in the train car, having seemingly teleported himself behind them. Before Jamie can even regain proper footing on the floor, the ghost tackles them headlong out the doors. All three of them tumble out onto the wooden tracks. Sid rolls to a stop without any serious damage due to his armor, but Jamie takes a battering on the railroad ties. The kid has more than a few boogered up fingers and nasty abrasions.

The transient is not slowed.

"You don't want to die quickly?" he screams, grabbing Jamie by the ears. "Then die slowly!" Sid barely manages to put himself between Jamie's face and 600 volts of electric shock as the transient tries to force Jamie onto the third rail that supplies power to the trains. Sid pushes back and Jamie screams from being crushed between the two raging killers. Sid overpowers the transient, but the ghost kicks him right through Jamie and sends him reeling backwards to the edge of the ties. For a second, Sid teeters over a fifty foot fall into moving traffic on the street below. "Die! Die!" the transient screams, reaching again to force Jamie against the rail.

Sid goes over the edge of the railroad, snarling and cursing at the monster. He catches the end of a tie on the way down, and pulls himself back up to the tracks, but he's too late to save Jamie from the transient.

Only the transient has halted in place.

"No. Not now!" the ghostly menace howls into the wind. "I need more time!" Jamie crawls down the tracks to get away from the screaming monstrosity as it shrieks even more frantically. "Only a few more seconds! No!"

Then the transient is gone.

Sid glances up and down the tracks. He looks over the edge to see if this is some kind of trick and the thing is about to come at him from somewhere else. Nothing. There's nothing up here but him, Jamie, and the rustling of the Chicago wind.

"Where did it go?" Jamie says.

"I don't know, but it didn't look happy about it," Sid says. "This is really fucking weird."

# EXT. BUCKINGHAM FOUNTAIN - NIGHT

"I'm never getting on the Green Line again," Jamie screeches while holding out a broken finger for Mary Sue to wrap in a makeshift splint. They made their way a few blocks east after falling off the train in an effort to ditch any police attention. After that, Sid used a phone he lifted from a parked car to call Bruce to meet up at the nearest large landmark.

"There's a reason the tourists don't ride that shit," Bruce says. The back of the utility van is packed with bright red cans and stinks of gasoline fumes.

"I don't think the reason is floating ghost assassins," Sid says. He is sitting on two of the gas cans for lack of room, packing ACP rounds into FNX magazines.

"Where do you think it went?" Bruce asks.

"Not a clue. He freaked out, screamed like he didn't want to go, and then he just poofed out of existence."

"He didn't leave anything behind? No pieces?" Mary Sue asks.

"Oh yeah, he left a couple arms, and a spare rib, and he pulled out his teeth and handed them to me— what the hell kind of pieces would he leave?"

"In the stairs where you blew that smoke grenade he was coughing up blood like he was sick. Some of it got on the handrail."

"Yeah? You think he's got AIDS or something? Good."

"Maybe, but that's not it. See I went back to the stairs later, and the blood was gone."

"Maybe it phased somewhere."

"I don't know, Sid. I'm not sure it was ever there to begin with."

"You're gonna have to explain this a lot better."

"What if we've been thinking about this all wrong from the start? What if the reason he can do all these things that seem impossible, is that he's not actually doing them?"

"Have you seen my face?" Jamie says, turning to display a deep black eye and lacerated forehead for Mary Sue to see more easily, not that she missed it before. The statement is rhetorical.

"I know. Sid, you compared him to a ghost when we first encountered him, and I dismissed that because I'm so stupid, but I think you were right."

"An actual ghost?" Bruce says. "Like Casper? He's a dead guy trapped in the world of the living?"

"No. I don't think that. But some fringe scientists theorize that reported poltergeist activity is caused by the overactive latent psychic abilities of people in close proximity. What if the transient is something like that? He could be using psychic powers to appear here, but from somewhere else. I know it sounds stupid, and I'm probably wrong . . . Just forget it. I'm so stupid sometimes."

"Hold up. That's maybe not as crazy as you think. In the '70s the company ran a whole bunch of experiments on that kinda shit. They'd hypnotize somebody and try to get 'em to astral project themselves into the Kremlin to spy on the Russians or find out what Castro had for breakfast or whatever."

"Right. That's called remote viewing, but it never worked. The government shut down the project in nineteen-ninety-five and all the documents were declassified. It's generally regarded as junk science now."

"Except you don't keep funding a program you know is bullshit for twenty years. That don't make sense."

"Have you paid any attention to the way our government works at all?" Jamie says. "They still fund abstinence only education."

"Yeah, well maybe I heard shit. I used to work for the CIA, you know. Maybe I heard that not all the files were declassified. Maybe I heard that the reason the project got canceled wasn't 'cause it didn't work, but because it worked too well. You ever think of that?"

"You heard that?"

"No. I'm just saying what if. You feel like a dipshit now?"

"No."

"I'm still having some trouble with this," Sid says. "You guys are saying the transient makes his ghost fly out of his body and run around on its own? And that's somehow more believable than he's just a guy who can walk through walls?"

"Not a ghost—a projection. He's affecting events in a remote location, but no part of him is actually present at that location. The apparition you see is an illusion—a type of hallucination. It explains everything if it's true. It's why he leaves nothing behind, brings nothing with him, flies, teleports, moves through solid matter. He's not actually doing those things. He just appears to be doing them. You can't hit him because he's not really there."

"I hit him in the stairwell. I punched him right in his stupid face."

"Oh." Mary Sue's head sinks, crestfallen. "I'm sorry. This whole idea was stupid. I'm so stupid. . ."

"I still think she's on to something," Player calls out in his weird computerized Stephen Hawking voice.

"Player?" Sid says. "How long have you been listening to this conversation?"

"I dialed him a while ago," Bruce says.

"What the fuck? Make noise or something."

"If the transient is a remote viewer, ostensibly a super charged one, we don't know the limits of that power. It does seem like he can't go without appearing as some sort of manifestation or another, otherwise he would remain invisible and Jamie would already be dead. Right? Maybe his form is what he thinks he looks like, and he can't unthink it."

"Like a residual self-image," Bruce says. "From *The Matrix*."

"So he's flying around believing he's in this body that you see, and believing he's picking up knives, and believing he's pushing Izumi Saito out of a window. Whatever he believes is what happens. If he believes Sid is punching him in the face, then Sid is punching him in the face."

"Like in *The Matrix*."

"Yes, Bruce. Like in *The Matrix*. Something we're talking about was actually related to *The Matrix*. Are you happy now?"

"Yeah."

Sid is growing impatient with all this theorizing. It doesn't seem to be getting them closer to the only thing he actually wants to know. "So if you guys are even anywhere close to right about all this, how do we kill him?" Sid says.

"His real body has to be somewhere," Bruce reasons. "We find it and shoot him like anybody else."

"Bruce, you just made me the happiest man on Earth."

"Aight. So we make a milk run back to the warehouse, burn down the apocalypse computer, then we figure out where the transient's real body is and we cap the bitch. Sound good?"

Mary Sue flinches as her cell phone buzzes and chirps a default ringtone. The noise is surprising, as she is only carrying a burner cell Bruce picked up from a grocery store. No one outside this van should have the number. She slides the burner from the waistband of her shorts and answers with a meek "Hello?"

Sid looks on with simmering disdain as she listens to what the other party has to say. He already knows what's coming.

"It's for you," Mary says. Of course it is. This stupid shit always happens. Sid takes the phone as Mary tells him what he already guessed. "It's Helen Anderson."

"How did you get this number?" he grumbles into the microphone.

"It's called a stingray, Sid," replies a very annoyed and slightly southern sounding female voice. Helen

Anderson is, since Sid last checked, the agent at the absolute top of Graveyard. "You should Google it."

"Google yourself," Sid says.

"Sounds like the quip clip is all out of bullets. Before you hang up, why don't you take a look out the back of that van?"

Sid already knows what he'll see, because he hears the rising cadence of war drums far off in the distance, so low that even he can barely make it out. He pops the back door anyway and takes a peek outside. He sees two black shapes growing in the northwest sky like giant insects over the big stone fountain. Choppers. More specifically, AH-64 Apache gunships—flying battle tanks equipped with a staggering array of missiles and guns, as well as an advanced targeting computer capable of directing all that explodey power at multiple targets with precision accuracy from miles away.

"I have two chain guns and one-hundred-fifty-two Hydra missiles locked on to your van," Helen says.

"Those chain guns are beyond effective range."

"I think we both know that's beside the point."

"What do you want?"

"I'll have somebody there in two minutes to pick up you and your friends. Let's have a chat."

# EXT. SIKORSKY CHOPPER - NIGHT

Mary Sue slouches timidly next to Bruce as he smokes his skinny little cigar. A Graveyard operator tried to tell him not to smoke in the helicopter, but Bruce told him to suck a donkey cock and lit it up anyway.

Sid is currently engaged in a staredown with Fleabag. The werewolf apparently acquired some fresh clothes since they last met, but he still has a few visible scrapes and bruises, and a single full-sized canine fang juts crookedly from his mouth even though he is in his human form.

"So is that like a werewolf fashion statement, or just a snaggletooth?" Sid says.

Fleabag refuses to break eye contact. He silently reaches up to his mouth, clutches the fang between two fingers and rips it out with its roots. He never blinks. The tooth drips blood for a second before he throws it from the open helicopter door.

"This is beyond toxic," Jamie says. "This is nuclear masculinity. This is A-bomb level."

"Whatever," Sid grunts, continuing to glare into the werewolf's eyes.

"Jiminy jillickers!" Bruce says, his cigar nearly falling from his mouth. "That's a god-damned battleship!"

Sid still won't look away from Fleabag, but he takes Bruce at his word. A minute later the chopper has set down on something and the rest of the passengers are hopping out of the cabin as the rotors spin down.

"The director's waiting for you right there," Fleabag says.

"I bet she is," Sid snarls back. They are already the only ones left in the back of the Sea Hawk. "After you."

"After you."

Neither of them budges.

"These seats are real comfy," Sid says.

"Sure are."

"So do you have a regular dick? Or one of those red rocket things?"

"Why don't you suck it and find out?"

"Man, you're crazy, Fleabag," says a nervous sounding Graveyard operator from the chopper skid.

"Crazy like a fox," Fleabag replies, intensifying his glare at Sid.

"You say that too?" Sid says, unfettered. "How does that make sense? How is a fox crazy?"

"It's just an expression. People use expressions."

Helen Anderson stomps aboard the chopper, blocking the sight line between them with her body. "This is ridiculous," she shouts. "You're both acting like macho assholes. This isn't *Top Gun*. Get off the chopper."

Fleabag growls, hops from his seat, and jumps down from the chopper. Sid shifts his eyes after the werewolf, looking out onto the aft deck of an Arleigh Burke class destroyer where the others are already waiting surrounded by uniformed navy men and Graveyard operators.

"I always thought *Top Gun* was really gay," Bruce says, standing just outside the chopper.

"What?!" Helen snaps back at him. "That's crazy."

"Nah, it's pretty gay. I mean you got Tom Cruise, gay, playing beach volleyball with oiled up dudes, gay, singing showtunes in a bar, gay, going on and on about how he loves some other dude, gay. . ."

"Goose? Goose died!"

"Plus there's this weird beta thing how Tom Cruise is all in love with an older woman who's just slightly dykey."

"Kelly McGillis is not dykey!"

"Kelly McGillis is a full-on lesbian!" Bruce yaps. He whips his attention to Jamie, and more than a few of the others follow. "Jamie, isn't Kelly McGillis a lesbian?"

"How should I know?" Jamie shrieks angrily. "Why are you all looking at me?"

"You got the gaydar, don't you? Or is that just regular gays?"

Helen rakes her long dusty blonde hair with frustration. "I can't imagine why a real government agency ever had you on the payroll."

"It's a long story," Bruce says.

Helen walks them from the helicopter pad under a towering overhead bay door and into a hangar behind the aft deckhouse. Sid guesses this is where they wheel the helicopter when they're not using it. The whole group remains under escort by eight operators who all seem a little shaky, and Fleabag, who does not seem shaky. Graveyard operators don't have uniforms per se, but they have guidelines. They always seem to wear black outfits, sometimes dark BDU's that stand out from modern ACU's which are always cam patterned and never black. Now they're wearing black Propper polo shirts and whatever pants happened to be clean. This is how they dress when they're trying to blend in with people in a populated area—minus all the subguns and tactical vests. Most of them have dark sunglasses. One guy actually has on an ACH helmet over his polo shirt, which looks out of place and makes Sid wonder if he donned that thing just for this special occasion. Kill Team One is going to be here; better put on a helmet. Weird.

A Navy officer wearing a rainbow of colored patches that mean nothing to Sid waits just inside the hangar door with a nervous smile. "Welcome aboard the USS John Milius," she says. "I'm Master Chief Wallace."

"Master Chief?" Bruce says. "Like *Halo?*"

"No," the Master Chief answers with a downtrodden frown. "It's not like *Halo*. It's never like *Halo.*"

"What kind of ship is this?" Mary Sue asks.

"The Milius is an Arleigh-Burke class guided missile destroyer."

"She should be safe on the ship from whatever is trying to kill her," Helen says, motioning to Jamie, clearly unaware of the internet blogger's nuanced gender status.

"She's not female," Sid grumbles.

Helen appears surprised. "Oh. He's trans? You're trans? I'm sorry—I didn't know."

"No. I'm actually non-binary," Jamie says.

"Oh. I see," Helen says, visibly struggling with this information. "What is that?"

"It's something else." Sid shakes his head. "It's like an in-between thing."

"What? Well, does he . . . or she . . . have . . . you know . . . which way were you originally?"

"Neither."

"You don't want to go down this road," Sid says. "I tried and I just got a headache. Whatever it is, it's infuriating."

"I can't understand how my gender identity is A, infuriating, and B, any of your business."

"It's my business because I don't know what words to call you to avoid an hour long metaphysical discussion."

"I already told you. You say they. It's they. That's not so hard!"

"That doesn't work! It sounds like I'm talking about a group of people."

"They call you Kill Team One! That sounds like a group of people too!"

"They's got you there," Helen says.

"It should be they've," Mary Sue corrects.

"Oh, God. Sid's right. That sounds weird. It's like I'm talking about somebody else. It's the hypothetical they then. They're watching. They've got this new diet. They say eggs are healthy for you. I could be talking about anybody. It's so unspecific."

"I wanted to pull its pants down right away and get this sorted out," Sid says. "Bruce stopped me, so you can blame him."

Jamie points angrily at Fleabag. "He turns into a ten foot wolf-man and you deal with that just fine!"

"Yeah. Wolf-*man*," Sid barks back. "*Man* is the operative word there. It leaves zero ambiguity. Fleabag, what do you call a girl werewolf?"

Fleabag raises a cheek as he considers the answer, then says "A hot mess."

"Heard that," Bruce chuckles.

"I hate all of you," Jamie says.

"So this is a super nice battleship," Mary Sue loudly proclaims to put an end to the argument.

"Yeah," Bruce agrees. "Did you guys buy or lease?"

"It's a rental," Helen says.

"Damn. I heard of Enterprise, but I didn't know you could get *The* Enterprise at Enterprise. It got one of those big glass world maps like they always have on the nuclear submarine in the movies?"

"It's called a vertical plotting board," Helen says. "And no. Nobody uses those anymore."

"Aw," Bruce grumbles. "I always wanted to be in one of those rooms."

"What about in the CIA? You know what—never mind." Helen physically shakes away the remains of that conversation. "Who wants to start?"

"Start what?" Sid says. "Aren't you starting?"

"Okay, fine. Why the hell are you here?"

"Why the hell are you here?"

"One of us has to actually answer the question."

"I don't have to do anything." Sid folds his arms in cold indifference.

"Then we're all going to stay very confused until whatever happens happens."

"I don't want to find out what happens," Jamie says.

"I need to know why forces unknown are attempting to kill Chan," Helen says.

Sid laughs. "That's the thing we don't know either! Nobody knows. Fuck it. I guess this was a waste of time. Everybody back in the helicopter."

"You stay right there, smartass," Helen sneers. "How did you get sucked into this?"

"That would be my fault," Bruce says. "See, I heard Chan call the Conspiratalk show, and me and Sid figured out it wasn't just a phony call on account of Chan said postmodernism and you said postmodernism was an end of the world scenario."

Helen's eyes shift up into her head as she recollects that previous conversation. "Because I told him about that last time we talked."

"You were here before the phone call," Sid says. "So how did you know?"

"Those internet bloggers were all part of a watch list. Some flags were raised when they started turning up dead."

"A watch list?" Jamie says. "I'm on a watch list? What for? What kind of watch list?"

"Classified." Helen eyeballs Jamie suspiciously. "How did you all make the connection?"

"They all worked on BuzzWorthy's doomsday machine," Sid snorts. "Duh."

"The what?!" Helen skeptically interjects. "They built a doomsday machine? BuzzWorthy?" She's on the verge of laughing at the idea.

"Yeah. The transient called it a codification mainframe. It brainwashes everybody into wearing these stupid pants with big fat legs."

"That's not what it does," Jamie whines. "This is so hard to explain. See, objective truth is a lie. The only thing that really matters is. . ."

"I know what a codification mainframe is," Helen interrupts, surprising everyone. "You can stop." She turns her attention back to Sid. "Who's the transient?"

"He's the ghost assassin killing all the bloggers. Everybody thought he was me, except he looks nothing like me. Also he walks through walls, and flies, and teleports, and does some other stuff, but we're not sure he's actually doing that stuff or if he's a remote viewer."

"A remote viewer? Like Project Stargate?"

"That's the one," Bruce says.

"Impossible. Remote viewers just view. That's why they're called viewers."

"So then there really are remote viewers?"

"Hmmm." Helen hesitates. "Not really."

"That hardly sounded definitive."

"It's complicated, but he's not a remote viewer."

"Do you have a better explanation?"

"No."

"He has some kind of serial number tattoo on his wrist," Sid says. "It says Aqua Six One Six Green."

"Really?" This piques Helen's interest. She hollers for one of her people. "Hey Dave." Dave is a pasty man with greasy hair and a tight-fitting pale green cardigan. He's the only one of Helen's entourage who doesn't look like he experiences regular bouts of 'roid rage. "Can you run a search for wrist barcodes with six-digit serial numbers, and anything along those lines? Cross reference with human experiments."

"Remote viewers," Bruce adds as Helen scribbles the barcode down for the analyst.

"He's not a remote viewer."

"What system am I searching?" Dave asks.

"All of them," Helen says.

"Ah. Okay. That'll take a while."

"I know." She stares at the analyst as he lingers for a quiet moment of awkwardness. Helen has to wave him off to get him moving. "Thanks, Dave," she says as he hurries off. Something occurs to Sid in the interim that does not add up.

"You knew about the bloggers," he says. "But you didn't know about the doomsday device."

"It's not a doomsday device," Jamie proclaims loudly.

"It's a doomsday device," Bruce argues.

"It's not a doomsday device," Helen says, rolling her eyes.

"It's not?" Jamie emits in high pitched surprise. Jamie *did* think it was a doomsday device then. Sid raises an eyebrow of annoyance at that implication.

"No," Helen assures. "We've had mainframes like that since the '80s. How do you think Rihanna ever got popular? It definitely wasn't her voice."

"Oh good," Mary Sue breathes a sigh of relief. "I thought I was tone deaf."

"Nah," Bruce says. "Rihanna sounds like an auto-tuned Dalek."

"You know how when you talk into a box fan it echoes back at you?" Fleabag offers. "I think she sounds like that."

"That's exactly what she sounds like!" Helen excitedly agrees.

"So nobody here likes Rihanna's voice?" Sid asks. Everyone present responds with a gesture of negativity, from headshakes to thumbs down to Bruce making a fart noise. Even Jamie, who originally exhibited Rihanna as a good singer, agrees that Rihanna sounds terrible. "So everybody just thinks that everybody else likes Rihanna's voice? How does that happen?"

"Codification mainframe," Helen says. "Of course, they usually don't work that well."

"Why? Why Rihanna?" Jamie says.

"Classified. All of this is classified. Not that anyone would believe you."

"She's right," Bruce says. "The evil shadow government conspiracy brainwashed everybody in the country to make some chick a popstar? That's the kinda shit crazy people say."

"Is it really?" Helen asks, slyly. "Or did we tell everyone to believe that?"

"Motherfucker. . ." Bruce stares off into empty space. "Don't you mess with my head like that."

"See?" Sid says. "I tried to warn you. Everything they touch turns to shit. We could have stayed home with Netflix and whores, but you guys had to save the world."

"Look, Jamie, I need know exactly who at BuzzWorthy actually built that machine," Helen asks.

"BuzzWorthy didn't build it," Jamie says. "I don't actually know who did. Maybe Izzy knew, but she's dead now. All of them are dead."

"You're telling me somebody else constructed a supercomputer of that caliber and just dumped it on you?"

"Good shit, isn't it?" Sid chuckles.

"Fuck!" Helen curses.

"The transient is probably one of his." Fleabag suggests. "Cleaning up the trail."

"Who?" Sid says. "What do you people know about this that you aren't saying? What's your interest here if there's no doomsday device?"

Helen scans the room for a suspicious second, lingering just a little too long on Jamie Chan. "Classified," she says.

"Okay, well clearly you guys have this all under control, so I'll just leave Chan with you and fuck off back to where I came from."

"You're stuck in this whether you like it or not," Helen says.

"Who says? You and the polo patrol? There aren't enough of you here to make me do anything."

"How are you going to get off the boat, Sid?" Helen questions skeptically.

"I'll swim," Sid grunts back. He might be able. Though he can't see the city anymore, so they must be pretty far out onto Lake Michigan.

"There's something you should see. Master Chief, can you show the others to the mess? We'll catch up with you."

# EXT. USS JOHN MILIUS - FO'C'SLE - NIGHT

"So what is it?" Sid grumbles as he looks up at the Mark 45 5-inch gun barrel over his head. The barrel points straight fore from a mount that appears something like an enormous grey cowbell behind Sid's back, and is enclosed in a red circle painted on the ship's deck to indicate all possible positions of the muzzle. Inside the circle is the safe zone. Outside the circle is the get-shot-by-an-actual-fucking-cannon-zone. Sid doesn't like that zone. Helen tried to walk out closer to the prow, but Sid refused to cross the line. He doesn't want to be in front of that gun. The damn things are automated. Most of the weapons on a ship like this are, and you just never know who's on the other end of the controls. So here they are under the gun barrel.

"There are details of this operation that can't be discussed in mixed company," Helen says. She has a laptop computer folded under her arm which she picked up in the ops room before they came out here. The forecastle is wide open, deserted, and inundated with the ambient noise of the ship and Lake Michigan. Helen couldn't have picked a better place to make sure no one is listening in—and that was certainly her intention. "We don't know which side everyone is on."

"It's Mary Sue, isn't it?" Sid looks over his shoulder suspiciously. "You can't trust anyone that nice. It isn't natural."

"No, smartass."

"I know. I'm being a dick on purpose."

"Sid, we don't know who Chan might be working with."

"I don't think Jamie is working with anybody, at least not in the sinister conspiracy sense. They might be working with a therapist, or working with an artist on a nice painting or something, but that's it. I spent a lot of time with that weirdo today. This is somebody who can't wrap their head around basic facts like whether they're a boy or a girl. Nobody like that has a head for espionage. Bruce practically had to draw a diagram to explain how the mystery player set them all up."

"What if that's all an act? Those other people from the watch list are all dead now—except for Jamie. Jamie can make up any story he or she wants. Isn't that a little too convenient?"

"We're not getting anywhere here. Cut the bullshit. What do you know about this that I don't?"

Helen unfolds the laptop from under her arm. "Here," she says, looking around the deck for the nearest place to set it down, but nothing is inside the gun's barrel radius, and even the couple of mooring posts and assorted railings along the edge of the deck would be ill-suited. "Don't they have a table or something out here?"

"Just-" Sid takes the laptop. "I'll just hold it."

"Okay, here." Helen reaches over his shoulder to manipulate the laptop. "It's in—oh great it went to sleep." She waits for the laptop to wake up and then it displays a large black screen which contains only a graphic of a vampire-fanged jolly roger and two empty fields for login and password. "Shit. It logged me out for inactivity. Just a second."

"Awesome." Already annoyed, Sid holds the laptop for Helen as she re-enters her password.

Helen grimaces at what appears on the screen. "Now it wants me to change my password."

"Seriously?"

"Yes, seriously. Even your average community college uses password rotations. You think the shadow government isn't as secure as the University of Phoenix Online?" Helen types some characters into the system and then rolls her eyes. "Oh for fuck—I need a non-letter or number character that I haven't used in the last twelve passwords."

"Try that straight up and down bar thing. Nobody ever uses that."

"The vertical bar? Good one. Let's see. Yeah. That works. Oh shit. Everything closed. Now I have to find the file again. Hang on." Helen enters a query into a search bar on the Graveyard system's home screen, which is not any friendlier than the login screen. "Okay got it." She presses enter.

Sid waits as an indicator appears on the screen with a percentage symbol. "It's buffering," he points out dryly.

"This is . . . You know I feel like these things always work until the second you try to show somebody something."

"Can you just tell me what it is?" Sid groans, tired of waiting for this stupid laptop to function correctly.

"You really need to hear it to believe it," Helen assures. The file's progress percentage meter finally begins gaining. "This transmission interrupted WGN for a minute and six seconds in nineteen-ninety-five during a broadcast of *Hercules: The Legendary Journeys*. Graveyard agents confiscated all known recordings. Our best analysts have listened to it and it has been run through every database the NSA has in search of patterns or connections to a current earthbound source and there isn't any. I think you'll understand right away why that's significant."

As the percentage indicator climbs, the audio begins to play. Sid is a block of solid skepticism, but as soon as he hears the first crackling words in a feminine pitch, an eerie chill creeps up his spine.

*I don't have much time. I don't know how far back this message will go, but I can tell you some things to try and prove I'm not making this up. Somebody shoots John Lennon, in nineteen-eighty, I think. Oh, Snape kills Dumbledore! Google is a thing. Then nine-eleven. iPhone. It starts getting weird after that. There's nothing left now. Everyone is dead, or one of those zombies, or they joined the death cult, and it's too late to fix it. They're cutting through the door. There's no time. You need to believe me. I know Comfort Eagle is real! The postmodernists are going to deconstruct everything and everyone will die! Whoever you are, you have to find Kill Team One. No one else can stop Wyatt . . . Get away, you fucking cunt! Get away from me!*

From there, the audio degenerates into a cacophony of heavy breathing and cursing and shrill screams. After a few seconds of howling shrieks, it cuts out with the sudden rustle of someone smashing or tearing at the microphone. The eerie message is bothersome to Sid. One might say it even comes close to shaking him. It is certainly frightening in tone and content, and the sounds of someone being horrendously torn at the end are quite graphic, but Sid has heard all those things before and typically yawns right through them. The detail that cuts to his core is not a gory one.

It is Lily Hoffman's voice in the recording.

Sid flares his nostrils and tightens his facial structure with intense thought. None of this makes sense. What could Lily possibly have to do with any of this top secret shit . . . in the future? Why would she have access to a time machine? Why would somebody fake this?

"It doesn't make sense," Sid grumbles to Helen with snarling incredulity.

"What part of it?" Helen wags her head at him with a sneering look that calls him an idiot without actually saying it.

"What's Comfort Eagle?"

"It's a song recorded by the band Cake in two-thousand-one."

Sid's face turns to deadpan stone as he glares through her for tossing him such an obvious lie by omission. "What is it really?"

"It's the Order's codification mainframe. It makes whatever BuzzWorthy has look like a pocket calculator."

"Who's Wyatt?"

"We're not exactly sure."

"Care to elaborate?"

"The recording was originally believed to be a prank by some insider with knowledge of the Comfort Eagle system. Graveyard combed for the perpetrator until someone realized Google was a search engine in ninety-nine. After the trade center even the most skeptical analysts agreed that the message was authentic. So they started looking for Wyatt. For years they came up with nothing at all. Most of the analysts were beginning to think the message was wrong, but recently they discovered some oddities."

"Oddities? What are oddities?"

"Weird stuff I can't really get into because I don't understand it that well myself. You have to understand the codification agents that run Comfort Eagle are really advanced, Sid. These guys very successfully manipulate the masses with song lyrics and blockbuster movies. It's a level of psy-ops that most of us can't comprehend. They cause shifts in birth rate, unemployment, violent crime, church attendance, all kinds of things that would surprise you. They're also mostly pretty strange. They make a big deal out of things like words with no etymological roots, or toy fads people remember for toys that never existed. A bunch of them are obsessed with finding a fake video game called Pollybevis—or something. I always say it wrong."

"Nerds."

"Oh yeah. Mega nerds. The nerdiest nerds. I don't think a one of them has ever gotten laid before. Anyway, these nerds pointed all their nerd computers at the internet and found a bunch of stuff they say doesn't add up. There are anomalies in the culture that could only have been caused by some artificial means other than them. They also say there's a strong pattern in the language at the origin of the anomalies."

"Huh?"

"The agents think there's a person, one person, somewhere out there in the country, causing all the anomalies."

"Wyatt."

"Yes. If the agents are right, Wyatt or whoever he is, is single handedly changing or undoing any programming he wants to. He's working against them, and it looks like he's winning, which is supposed to be impossible."

"You think Jamie might be Wyatt? Is that what you're getting at here?"

"Sid, the codifiers created a profile along with a list of likely suspects—the watch list. Jamie is the only one left alive."

"Except that Jamie says somebody else built that machine and Bruce thinks that was all just a setup. That sounds more like your evil mastermind."

"The transient is the key to this now. We need to find out why he thinks Jamie is so dangerous. What's his evidence? Either he's wrong, or he knows better than we do and he's trying to kill Jamie and prevent the apocalypse."

"Sounds like fifty-fifty odds on the end of the world." Sid shrugs. "Good luck with that. You don't need me."

"You heard Lily! She said only you can stop Wyatt!"

"You can't believe anything Lily says. You don't know her. She's a lying skankbox."

"It's a message from the fucking future!"

"Well if you want to test all this shit, it's not hard. Call down to Fleabag and tell him to shoot Chan in the brain stem right now. If Chan is Wyatt then it won't work. The bullets will bounce off or something."

"She said only you can *stop* Wyatt. It's not the same thing as killing him. It could be that if someone else kills Wyatt instead of you, that's what causes the apocalypse."

"I don't think that's what she meant."

"I don't know. She's your girlfriend."

"She's not my girlfriend. And how do I know you didn't call her up and record this thing just to get me to come work for you?"

"That would be awfully elaborate. Don't you think?"

"I think you want me back that bad."

"Oh please. Your ego is unbearable. I have companies of commandos and a whole other team that can do what you do."

"Yeah? What's that kill team called? What number are they?" Graveyard never re-numbered the kill teams even after Sid vanished. He has found that interesting for some time, and it seems like a good item to rub in Helen's face.

"For your information, we don't call them kill teams anymore. They're Guardians."

Sid almost felt rebuffed until he heard the new name. Now he has to laugh. "That's a stupid name for a death squad."

"They're not a death squad."

"Right. They fly in on a helicopter and kill people on your orders. I totally see your point now. That in no way resembles a death squad."

"We just don't call it that, Sid."

"I'm not Sid anymore. Now they call me Loverboy. I woo the ladies with my charms and romance and stuff."

"You know, this is interesting. Wyatt is apparently a postmodernist, which is all about the end of universal objective truths. You're supposed to kill Wyatt, and you're the most objective person I've ever met. You're practically like an animal."

"Don't try to fight it, Helen. Now that I'm Loverboy you find me irresistible."

"I would rather let a dog hump me."

"Woof."

"Are you gonna help us or not?"

# INT. USS JOHN MILIUS - MESS - NIGHT

The ship's messdeck—which is a lunchroom—is a blue tile floored space containing fifteen tables, a row of drink dispensers, a small salad bar, some mounted televisions, and a hardwired phone tucked neatly away in the back corner. Everything is bolted to the floor—which is called a deck. Bruce sinks into a hard metal seat and pops the top from a can of Grape Crush he acquired from a vending machine in the hallway—only they're not called hallways. They're called p-ways, because everything on a ship has to have a weird fucking name that doesn't make sense. The Master Chief seems to love pointing these things out. She does it politely, like a helpful tour guide, but Bruce still thinks it's dumb. He was glad when she went off to her office or somewhere and left them alone.

Across the thick blue tablecloth, Fleabag peels the wrapper from the last of a stack of beef sticks he obtained from the vending machines as well. He does so blindly as he's staring over his shoulder at Mary Sue and Jamie while they (meaning both of them) investigate a cappuccino machine near the entryway. Bruce can't decide if that's called a door or a hatch. There's no way it's just a door. It's probably not a hatch either. They probably call it a walkhole or something equally goofy.

"So what's going on with pinky over there?" The werewolf picks up all ten unwrapped sticks of jerky in a bundle and bites through them, chewing and bearing his teeth the way Bruce would expect a carnivorous dinosaur to eat. The mess is hardly crowded, but there are a few sailors occupying the other tables, and Fleabag clearly isn't the only one paying attention to the voluptuous female figure in the sea of seamen. Guys were rubbernecking at her all the way from the weatherdeck, although she remained completely oblivious, as always. "What's her . . . situation?"

"She's sixteen," Bruce answers.

"That is a situation." Fleabag stretches his mouth into a wry expression. "I think I can wait."

"Never mind what's going on with her. What's going on with you?" Bruce says. "You turn into a werewolf. That's some shit. How's that happen?"

"Either you get bit by a werewolf or your parents are werewolves." Fleabag chomps more beef jerky.

"No shit?"

The werewolf notices a sailor two tables over staring at him as he chews the jerky, probably because it is a bit of a spectacle. "What are you looking at, Popeye?" The sailor quickly buries his eyes in his own plate of food. "That's what I thought."

"So I'm guessing you eat a ton of meat," Bruce says.

"Around ten pounds a day. It costs a fucking fortune."

A sudden quiet and a lot of swiveling heads causes Bruce to turn his attention back toward the rear of the mess, where a crusty grey hand has erupted from the bulkhead in the middle of a painted crest displaying the ship's name and motto: *With extreme prejudice!*

The hand is followed by a horrific face, empty-eyed and rotten, but far worse than before. The left quarter of the transient's face is now completely open to the inside of his cranium, which is stuffed with darkness that seeps out into the air like a black flame.

"There you are!" the monster says again, pointing halfway across the mess to where Jamie Chan is dumping sugar packets into a cup of coffee.

"That's him!" Bruce shouts, pointing back at the transient. "How the fuck he find us on a motherfucking boat?!"

Fleabag is already growing in size, both because he is standing from his seat, and because he is shifting into a snarling man-wolf. Jamie screams and drops the coffee on the deck of the mess deck before bolting for the door. Nine tenths of the sailors follow. One guy pulls a gun. A few others seem to be fixed in place by their buckling sanity. A culinary specialist behind the salad bar looks on like he's watching Katie Morgan wrestle six midgets naked. The sailor currently utilizing the mess's satellite phone shakes his head and shouts into the mouthpiece.

"Baby, there's a werewolf and a ghost in the messdecks!"

The werewolf hits his head on the low ceiling and has to duck down to stomp toward the wall phasing menace. The guy with the pistol shoots Fleabag in the side twice before realizing he's being retarded and also running for the door. Fleabag doesn't seem to notice the bullet wounds as he pounces on the transient, but he just goes right through the ghostly creature and slams into the bulkhead behind it.

The transient floats through the mess, listing from side-to-side, and shouting after Jamie. "You can run no longer! My killing intent is uncaged, unfiltered, pure!" Fleabag rakes his hefty talons through the transient's back twice, but is ignored. The transient floats out of the mess through the door with the werewolf biting and clawing at him all the way. Left alone with a stunned Mary Sue and very entertained cook, Bruce gets up from his seat.

"What do we do?" Mary Sue says. Bruce throws his hands up in the air as he walks after the werewolf and the phantom. There doesn't seem to be much reason to hurry, as he can do nothing useful even if he catches up to them. Mary Sue dashes too enthusiastically past him after the monsters.

The culinary specialist shakes his head. "White people. . ."

"Type shit," Bruce mutters back, on his way from the mess.

An alarm klaxon sounds throughout the ship as Bruce creeps down the narrow corridor.

"Security alert, security alert! Away the security alert team! Away the back-up alert force! All hands not involved in security alert stand fast! There is a. . ." the speaker stalls momentarily. "There is a problem." Bruce doesn't know what else to call it either.

Down the p-way, the werewolf scrapes onward, filling up the narrow space more than a little bit like a sci-fi movie blob. He's just way too big to move around the inside of this ship. He has to go through a door on all fours, and even then barely squeezes through. Bruce can't see past the moving wall of fur to see what the transient is doing. Mary Sue trails only a few feet behind Fleabag, unable to move beyond him.

From behind Bruce, someone shouts a husky warning. "Out of the way!" It comes from a sailor wearing a body armor vest over his uniform and carrying an old-school M16A1 rifle with the full buttstock. Bruce can't figure where he came from. The ship is a labyrinth of narrow twists and turns all packed with pipes and cables and ladders. Navigating it is like trying to trace a single strand of spaghetti through a bowl. Another sailor appears behind the first and raises his rifle as soon as he sees the monster ahead.

Bruce starts to tell him to stop, but then realizes nothing he can say in less than ten minutes will help anyone here, so he just throws himself against the deck and screams at Mary Sue. She plasters herself against the nearest bulkhead and the sailors start shooting. The automatic rifles make an ungodly amount of racket in the enclosed p-way, and the only real damage they manage to do is to Bruce's eardrums. Being shot by dozens of rifle rounds just makes the werewolf angry.

"You guys are shooting at the wrong monster!" Bruce shouts from the floor. "Hold your fucking fire!"

"Stay down!" A sailor screams back, ramming another magazine into the M16 in his hands. Down the p-way, the werewolf pushes himself toward the ceiling and Jamie Chan dives between his spread ankles, apparently having reversed direction somewhere ahead.

"Hold your fire!" Bruce shouts. Mary Sue pushes herself up from the deck and chases Jamie back toward them.

"Shut up!" the sailors shout, even though they refrain from firing down the p-way just as Bruce insisted. Jamie hoofs it past Bruce as he stands back up from the deck. The transient floats right through the werewolf, looking even angrier than ever before. Bruce throws himself down again as the sailors open fire on the transient.

Bullets zip through the transient with no effect, but rip into the werewolf behind it, shredding muscle and furry flesh. Another fang cracks from the monster's snout and clatters to the deck with bloody drool as it struggles forward through the tiny p-way.

The transient stops and reaches for one of the sailors' guns, but the man yanks it violently away.

"Give me that!" he bellows, inky black fog rising from his mouth the way warm breath is visible in the cold, only whatever is leaking from him is totally impenetrable. He reaches for the other sailor's weapon. "Feel my void!" he roars, blackness streaming from his gaping mouth and hollow eyes in a cone of vile dark that projects right through the sailors like they're made of tissue paper.

Both men scream wildly. One of them begins crying and firing his gun at the ceiling. The other deep throats the muzzle of his M16 with immediacy so furious that it disturbs Bruce more than the visage of both monsters, and probably more than anything else he has ever seen before. Bruce is convinced that guy absolutely could not wait to blow his own brains out. It was like a suicide race and he had to be the winner, and nothing else in the world mattered more.

"What the fuck?" Bruce mutters. "I didn't know he could do that. Did you know he could do that?" he asks of Mary Sue, on the floor a few feet away, a little closer to ground zero of whatever that was that the monster did. She has a glassy-eyed gaze that Bruce has never seen from her before.

"I saw people hurting puppies," she says. "Why were they hurting puppies?" Bruce grabs Mary Sue's nearest wrist and pulls her toward him as soon as it becomes apparent that the girl ain't right. They need to get the hell away from that thing—whatever it is. Fuck this. Fuck saving Jamie Chan.

The transient already has scooped up the dead man's rifle and is firing after Jamie down the p-way in the opposite direction. Bullets skitter and ricochet loudly down the corridor as Bruce pulls Mary Sue into the moving wall of bloody meat that is the werewolf. Fleabag shrinks back to a human shape so they can pass. Bleeding from a dozen gunshot wounds, he tugs the suspenders that hold up his oversized pants and follows along behind them.

"It's like it's not even there," Fleabag says. "I couldn't touch it!"

"That's what we told you before!" Bruce barks back, looking down the p-way ahead, unable to see anything that looks like an end to it. There are some cramped stairs just ahead and to his right, so he takes them. There isn't a great reason. He just has an irrational feeling that he needs to put walls between him and whatever just happened. A floor will do just as well.

He takes one last look back down the p-way behind him and sees the remaining sailor mercilessly beating his forehead bloody against the deck, squealing like a pig, and repeating "I don't want my eyes! I don't want my eyes!"

Helen Anderson is at the top of the steps to offer Bruce a hand. She is quickly joined by several more armed sailors. "Bruce! Did you see where it went?"

"Fuck it!" Bruce says, walking Mary Sue up to the next deck. "This ship don't have enough guns to put that thing down."

"Those poor puppies," Mary Sue whimpers. "He isn't from now. We think he's from now, but he's not."

"What's wrong with her?" Helen says.

"I think she saw into the motherfucker's deadlights or some shit. I don't know. She didn't get it as bad as the security guards."

"That's him!" shouts a sailor coming toward them with even more armed guards. "That guy turned into the monster!"

Three sailors from the security response team slam an annoyed Fleabag to the deck and pile on top of him despite Helen's loud protestations. "He's with me! Stop that! Where's Captain Willard?"

# INT. USS JOHN MILIUS - BERTHING - NIGHT

Sid stalks the aft p-ways of the main deck like a jungle cat, only he's a jungle cat with a submachine gun. He borrowed the MP5 from Helen's operators after he begrudgingly agreed to help them. He had to agree. It was the only way off this stupid boat. Incidentally, it does seem like the rest of them are in over their heads without him in this whole postmodern apocalypse situation. He half cares about that—sort of. He told Helen to get a boat ready for him and left her at the front of the Milius as soon as he heard the alarms. Hopefully these sailors will be able to get that shit together in decent time so he doesn't have to stall.

It doesn't take him long to get an idea where the transient went. He only has to go the opposite direction of all the running sailors whose reactions range from terrified hysteria to mildly skeptical caution. Shuffling around them in the tight space proves incredibly obnoxious. When one sailor gets in Sid's face for going the wrong way, the kill team gives him a one-way ticket to Concussionville with an elbow to the jaw.

"I don't have time for this," Sid grumbles.

He gets a glimpse of the blackened creature another dozen meters down the p-way. The thing looks like it went through a meatgrinder since the last time he saw it. Half its head is an empty hole now. It is armed with an M16A1 rifle, the older variety that fires full auto and has a full-size barrel and stock. It's weird to see the transient walking around with a gun rather than floating, but it makes sense. He needs some kind of weapon to do his job. The creature doesn't see Sid, nor does Sid make his presence known before it vanishes around another corner.

"Where are you hiding, hedonist?" the transient's voice echoes over the buzz of the ship's machinery. "There are barbarians at the gate and you can't wait to lower the drawbridge!"

When Sid comes around the corner, he sees the transient's horrid form hovering between sets of racks—flat bunk beds made from sheets of aluminum and stacked three high. They might more accurately be described as slots or cubbies to common soft Americans unfamiliar with the cramped conditions on a warship. Compared to the comforts the first world knows, these might as well be morgue drawers, but Sid can appreciate the austerity of it all.

The racks have short blue privacy curtains, but only two are pulled closed out of the nine bunks visible. The transient points his gun at one of the curtains and balances the weapon in one hand as he reaches for the blue fabric with the other.

"Are you . . . in here?" he rips back the curtain to reveal an empty rack. He excitedly blasts the M16 into the padding at his fingertips. The rifle jumps wildly in his right hand until he releases the trigger looking astonished. The wide-eyed monster gives pause then, as if he's never fired a fully automatic weapon before. Process of elimination puts Jamie hiding in the other curtained off rack, behind the transient, and Sid is out of ideas for extracting the journalist safely from that situation.

It's time for that other smoke grenade. He pitches the grenade into the berthing quarters and it sails right through the transient's head trailing a purple plume. The transient spins viciously to confront Sid, screaming his banshee scream and blasting wildly with that rifle as smoke quickly envelopes him and pours through the door where the kill team is waiting. Bullets clatter against the bulkheads as Sid takes cover outside the doorway. The transient's gun runs dry and the monster bellows an angry curse as Sid dives blindly into the berthing racks. He doesn't make it four feet into the room before he hears the slapping of hands on the deck amidst this haze. Sid reaches for the sounds and fills his hand with a clump of hair, too long to belong to a sailor. He pulls aggressively and yanks Jamie Chan out into the p-way.

The internet blogger slaps at his hands in a panic until they are clear of the smoke, meters down the corridor.

"Follow me," Sid barks. Now that he has located and retrieved Chan, he has a plan in place for escape.

"How did it get here?" Jamie says. The question would be sensible under normal circumstances, and even now it is not entirely uncalled for, considering they are in the middle of 22,000 square miles of featureless water. The only worthwhile takeaway is that they have now confirmed the transient can truly track Jamie absolutely anywhere.

"The same way it gets everywhere else," Sid growls back. He pulls Chan up a ladder into another p-way, then whips them both out through a port onto the weatherdeck where the Master Chief is waiting. The ship's loudspeaker blares behind them.

"General quarters, all hands battle stations."

"Is it ready?" Sid shouts at the Master Chief. She looks like a deer in the headlights as he tramples over her toward the railing and a collection of lines dangling toward the water. Sid takes a look over the railing, sees one of the destroyer's rigid-hulled inflatable boats in the water below, and heaves Chan overboard.

"Are you stupid?" the Master Chief screams.

"Stupid like a fox," Sid barks back, before leaping over the railing himself to plummet thirty feet to the boat below.

He pulls Jamie from the cold black water and starts the small boat's engine. In a few more seconds they're zipping away from the Milius at 40 knots toward the hazy illumination on the horizon that gives away the Chicago coastline. Sid looks back and sees a man-shaped shadow like a blackened cutout in the air between them and the searchlights of the big destroyer. He flips it a big finger as it shrinks into the darkness.

# INT. USS JOHN MILIUS - CIC - DAY

CIC on the John Milius is no more spacious than the rest of the ship, but it is much darker. The compartment itself isn't so tiny, but all the computer equipment packed into it hardly leaves any leg room, and the lights are turned down about as low as most MMORPG addicts would prefer. About the only thing in the room that is well-lit is the vertical plotting board, which is manned by a sailor with a black grease marker who is writing backwards on the flipside of the glass partition. Bruce badly wants to throw that in Helen's face, but now isn't the time. She's currently next to a ladder outside CIC, engaged in a discussion with the ship captain that includes a lot of fist shaking from both parties.

Bruce can only make out useless bits like "endangered my crew" and "onboard my ship." He gets the impression it's a fairly standard clash of command head-butting thing.

"I was so stupid," Mary Sue mumbles from the floor where she was tucked away next to a sailor manning a computer terminal featuring a rather unmistakable green-on-black radar display, complete with beeping blips and sweeping radial trace. They tucked Mary Sue away in this corner while the Navy secured—that's a laugh—secured the forward deckhouse and stuffed Fleabag away somewhere. Bruce doesn't think they have a brig on this ship. Maybe they do. It doesn't matter. It won't hold the werewolf any longer than he wants to stay.

"Honey, you're not stupid," assures the Master Chief. She offers Mary Sue some hot chocolate from the mess which the girl gingerly accepts.

"What did you see in there?" Bruce says, knowing that he's pushing his luck. He probably shouldn't ask too many questions just yet.

"Bad things," Mary Sue says. "It felt like all the bad things."

"You guys get anything out of that other sailor?" Bruce asks the Master Chief.

She shakes her head solemnly. "He's dead. He ran to the galley and stabbed himself in both eyes with a bread knife right after you saw him."

"Shit's deep."

Helen comes through the CIC door seconds later looking put-off. "Well, the captain wants us off the ship," she says, frowning slightly. "No surprise there. The good news is I don't think it makes much difference since the transient seems to be able to go wherever it wants anyway."

"I don't think that's exactly true," Mary Sue says. "Not the way you mean."

"Well he sure didn't swim here," Bruce says. "You care to elaborate?"

"He read somewhere that we would be here. I saw it—a website, or an email."

"That doesn't make sense. You think someone is emailing him directions?" Helen questions, giving off more than a hint of skepticism. "Then how does that person know where to find Jamie?"

"I know it sounds dumb." Mary Sue looks down at her hot chocolate in despair. "I'm so stupid."

Before Bruce can tell Helen to lighten up on the girl, Dave the dweeby Graveyard analyst pokes through the doorway look for her. "Director?" he says. "I've got something on that number."

"Great. Spill it. First good news all day," Helen says.

"Well there was nothing in any of the American records, or anything we stole from the Russians. Turns out that despite what you see in dystopian science fiction, it is actually quite unusual to tattoo human subjects with serial numbers. Plausible deniability is an issue. The logistics of tattooing large populations are also quite complicated. The Nazis did it at Auschwitz, but nowhere else, mostly because it was so unfeasible. So I gave up on black projects and checked out FBI and Interpol. I came up with something right here in our backyard."

"Indiana?"

"The other backyard. Canada. Last year in Toronto, an unidentified man entered a political rally and shot a regional council candidate to death in front of a hundred people. The killer had a three digit numeric code and two colors on the right forearm. Cerulean, five, eight, two, blue."

"That sounds a whole fuckin' lot like what we're looking for," Bruce says. "Weird tattoo, check. Motherfucker doing some prescient shit nobody can explain, check."

"Except the police shot that perpetrator dead within seconds of the assassination. The body was never identified."

"Great. So we're back to square one?" Helen says.

"Not exactly. I know you told me not to look at the remote viewing thing. . ."

"Oh no," Helen hangs her head in defeat. "What did you find?"

"Stargate was a dead end. No connections. What isn't so well known is that the British government ran their own remote viewing experiments long after the Americans gave up. The brits eventually shut their program down too, a few years ago. I checked out their personnel, and as it turns out, one of the senior researchers from that program now heads a mental health facility in Toronto Canada."

"You think this guy just moved his operation across the pond?"

"I know he did."

"How are you so sure?"

"Because we're sending him a lot more money than it costs to operate a mental health facility."

Helen groans. "This day just keeps getting worse."

Bruce laughs. "Graveyard is funding this shit and you didn't even know about it?"

"It's not that simple. Graveyard doesn't fund research programs. R&D does. It's a whole other department. This still doesn't add up. I mean the theory is ridiculous—a remote viewer is what? Astral projecting himself into some kind of monster?"

"You keep saying that, but the government is still playing this shit way too close to the chest for me to believe remote viewing is impossible. They still got all those documents they never declassified."

"That's not how it is, Bruce it's—I have access to all those records—even the redactions and the files that were officially lost. I've read through it extensively. They didn't cancel Stargate because remote viewing is impossible, per se. They cancelled the program because no useful information could be collected. That's not the same thing."

"Uh . . . Explain?"

"Remote viewers are on a spectrum. On one extreme you have the fakers—which is pretty much all of them, because the rarity of actual remote viewers is one in hundreds of millions. As you move up the spectrum, you start to see people who actually do have some ability. Maybe they can feel an area where something bad happened or get general reads of other people's concealed emotions. Those weaker abilities aren't useful for much. As you continue up the spectrum there are individuals who *can* see what playing card is in your pocket, or what song a radio DJ is about to play, or even Vladimir Putin's bedroom proclivities. The problem is they're crazy—and the stronger they get, the crazier they get. I don't understand why necessarily. I'm just telling you what I read, but they shut the program down because it was an immense waste of time and resources. They spent ninety-nine percent of their time interviewing simpletons and cold readers, and the viewers they found are bananas. They're loopy. Most of them were permanently committed after the program if they weren't already. Sure, they can technically see anything anywhere, but they're babbling incoherently most of the time. There isn't any way to discern if they're reciting nuclear launch codes or next week's Showcase Showdown prices. None of it was useful. Never mind at all that remote viewers just view. They don't appear like ghosts or push people out windows or do . . . whatever that thing does."

Helen's explanation is disturbed by the tinny sound of Toby Keith's *Courtesy of the Red, White and Blue* through her tiny cell phone speaker. She answer the phone hurriedly. "Who is this? Sid? Where are you?"

# INT. CHANEL BOUTIQUE - DAY

"I'm back on the fucking Mag Mile!" Sid Hansen snarls into a hardline phone over a glass case displaying two Chanel handbags near the center of a vast blank white space. It was the first structure he came to after emerging from the ocean, so he barged in, walked behind the counter and picked up the phone." I beached the boat, walked through a tunnel under the freeway, and now I'm back here! I fucking hate this place!"

"Sir," a wispy woman in a conservative black dress approaches Sid, extending her arm in an admonishing gesture. "Who let you use that phone? I'm afraid you need to leave the store."

Sid lowers the phone and glares at her with death flames burning in his eyes. "I do whatever the fuck I want." He points at the other end of the display counter, which stretches the length of the store. "Now shut the fuck up and go back over there before I hit you so hard it makes your children retarded."

The threat works with incredible immediacy. The shopkeeper stumbles backwards on the heels of her pumps. That should buy a few minutes. Jamie Chan wows at the reaction from the other side of the counter. "I can't believe that worked."

"She'll be back. They always think they can come back with help. They're always wrong." Sid puts the telephone back to his ear. "You guys still on the boat?"

"For now. We're being evicted as soon as the choppers get here. We might have a lead on that serial number you saw on the transient's arm. Bruce thinks it's promising, but I'm not convinced. There's something else you need to know. The transient can do something else. Something we didn't know about before."

"Like a handstand?"

"He shot black rays out of his eyes and made two sailors crazy. It reduced them to total psychotic breakdown. They killed themselves, Sid. I've never seen anything like it. Mary Sue was a few feet away when it happened and she's acting kind of loopy now."

"Loopy?"

"She was talking about dead puppies. We gave her some hot cocoa and now she's just saying a lot of stuff that doesn't really make sense. I don't think she'll be of much help for a while."

"Great. He has gibbering madness eyes. That just made my day so much better." It did not. It made Sid's day worse.

"Gibbering madness eyes?" Helen questions. "Is that a real thing? Or are you joking?"

Sid sees the huffy shopkeeper coming back his way and pointing him out to a dapper looking man with a waxy bald head. "I'm going to keep the ladyboy moving. I have to go now, or I'll have to shoot my way through the Chicago Police."

Sid hangs up the phone just as the bald headed Chanel manager opens his mouth. "Sir, you're not even close to glam enough to be in here. You need to leave."

Sid fractures this man's skull against the white paneling inside the display case. The glass might as well have been single-ply toilet paper he went through it so easily. Sid rips the telephone receiver from its outlet and throws the whole boxy plastic unit at the tattling shopkeeper. It sails five meters through the air and directly into her screaming face, where it crashes and cracks with a loud dinging. She flops off those heels and tugs one of the store's fine upholstered stools with her on the way to the ground. She doesn't get back up.

There is only one witness, a solitary early shopper who stands slack jawed at the far end of the beige carpeted show floor. Her Starbucks Pumpkin Spice Latte rattling in her well-manicured hand.

"You didn't see shit!" Sid growls, pointing from across the store.

"I didn't see shit," the shopper agrees.

"Good," Sid says. "Come on." He orders Jamie out the door behind him. They need to move quickly. Promises not to talk are rarely kept long, and someone else is likely to wander in here soon anyway. They head out into the street and turn the corner onto Michigan, heading for the subway station on Chicago and State.

"Did you just kill those people?" Jamie asks, still in a quiet state of shock.

"Nah," Sid dismisses the idea. "Those are just head injuries. Nothing a few months of painkillers and physical therapy won't fix." He moves on to the next topic without giving Jamie any time to process that information. "Here's the deal. The evil black helicopter guys have a message from the future that says somebody named Wyatt is going to cause the end of the world by doing the same kind of shit you're doing."

"Promoting transgender rights?"

"Sure. I guess. No? I don't know. I shoot people and blow stuff up. I don't really handle the philosophical bits too well. Anyway, the transient thinks you're Wyatt, and that's why he wants to kill you. Are you Wyatt?"

"No! That's insane! All of this is insane! What do you mean a message from the future? Like with a time machine or what?"

"Either that or they got my ex-girlfriend in on a really elaborate prank. Which do you think is more likely?"

"Time travel message from the future or ex-girlfriend prank? Uh . . . Ex-girlfriend prank."

"You haven't been doing this long enough. It's the time travel thing. That's definitely more likely."

"The New World Order thinks I'm this Wyatt too? Is that why I'm on a watch list?"

"Pretty much."

"I don't even know anyone named Wyatt!"

"Yeah. I told them you're not smart enough to be Wyatt, but I don't think they believe me."

"Thanks, I guess?"

"Anyway, we're all pretty sure whoever really built the codification engine for BuzzWorthy is the real Wyatt. I think if we can find him, we can sic the transient on him instead of you. Seeing as he's invincible, unstoppable, and can find you anywhere, that's pretty much your only hope. Too bad you don't have a clue. . ."

"The IP address Mary Sue found in the system!" Jamie belts out. "Do you remember it? You remember everything, don't you?"

"Yeah. I remember. You think it belongs to Wyatt?"

"It has to! Nobody else had access to the system that isn't already dead. I know a hacker who can trace that IP too!"

"Let's go see him."

"The only problem is I don't think he'll want to help us."

"Why not?"

"Because he's a terrible person."

"I think I can probably persuade him."

# EXT. THE VEIDT INSTITUTE - DAY

Bruce is in another helicopter packed with commandos again. He wonders where Graveyard gets these things—or rather how they get them so fast. This chopper, a Blackhawk, came and picked him up from the pad at the rear of the John Milius only an hour after Helen's argument with the ship's captain. Now they're zipping through Ontario with an apparently fake insane asylum framed in the cockpit window. When the chopper is almost over the building, Fleabag starts issuing commands to his operators.

The chopper touches down in a big square patch of frost covered grass in front of the main building, then disperses as soon as all of the hard-asses with automatic weapons have their boots on the ground.

Helen and Bruce follow the machine gun patrol up to the facility, which is an older three floor red brick building incorporating some stone work around the doors. A tapestry carved into one of those door frames identifies the building as a school, which it is not.

Fleabag is making hand motions directing his hard-asses where to enter the building when a man in a white lab coat marches somewhat unexpectedly through the front door with his hands up. He has a thick white beard like Santa Claus and a voice to match.

"Graveyard?" he shouts. "Come on in. We've been expecting you."

Obviously this guy has zero experience dealing with covert operator types, because that behavior just makes everyone think they're being led into a trap, and ten seconds later Dr. Santa Claus is face down on the ground wearing a lovely zip tie bracelet. Helen identifies him from his dossier photo while they're waiting for the fireteam to sweep the facility.

"That's Dr. Nolan Sartorius," she says. "He's the one we're looking for."

"I could have just told you that," the doctor grumps into the chilly grass while a black-clad commando pins a knee into his shoulder blades.

"Shut up!" the operator shouts.

"How did you know we were coming?" Helen asks.

"It's not like we were real subtle," Bruce snarks and points toward the drumming helicopter that waits for them nearby.

"One of the patients saw it happening," Sartorius says. "He's quite gifted."

"What the hell kind of experiments are you running in there, doc?"

"I'd be glad to show you. Perhaps you can order your jackbooted hooligan to release me and we'll go inside? I can put some tea on."

"We're going to take a raincheck on the tea party, Sartorious," Helen says. "My team is sweeping your horror house right now."

"This is all some kind of misunderstanding!"

"Shut up!" interrupts the jackbooted hooligan again.

A few minutes later, Fleabag emerges from the facility with another operator. The werewolf is hauling his M60 machine gun by its carry handle and he looks quite puzzled as he approaches the spot where Helen and Bruce have the good doctor detained.

"How bad is it?" Bruce says. "They got half human mutants floating in tubes with all kinda wires and shit connected to 'em?"

"No," Fleabag shakes his head.

"Mind control collars? Robot security guards?"

"No." Fleabag's reaction turns annoyed.

"Velociraptors with rocket launchers for arms?"

"No. And where would we ever see that?"

"I dunno." Bruce shrugs.

"Director," Fleabag addresses Helen in what Bruce reads as an attempt to brush aside his entire line of questioning. "I don't think this is the kind of place we thought it was when we flew in here."

# INT. THE VEIDT INSTITUTE - DAY

The first room inside the Veidt Institute is a long waiting room, exactly like a doctor's office waiting room, with the weird additional detail that there are even some large toys for young children strewn around the carpet among the variety of colored chairs that line the walls. An operator holding a CZ Scorpion with laser aiming module and suppressor stands guard over a terrified looking 20-something with her small child clutching an Elmo toy nearby. Another operator with a thick horseshoe mustache leans in the opposite corner, his eyes glued to a frozen middle-aged secretary, her hands high over her head as she stands behind the reception counter near the door.

Helen groans loudly as she enters the room and witnesses this spectacle. "Jesus Christ, Ned. I think we can safely assume Elmo isn't wearing a suicide vest."

"It's just you never know," the operator objects. "We've got Kill Team One involved in this, and it all gets so weird so fast when he comes around."

"That's exactly what he says about you guys," Bruce observes. "Y'all got to learn to communicate better." Bruce approaches the people in the waiting room with his hand out. "How you doin' bud?" he asks the little boy on the floor. The kid is quiet, and maybe a little uneasy, but not scared the way his mother is. Kids are like that. They can cry like the dickens over a spilled ice cream but put them in a room full of armed soldiers with questionable intentions and they just don't know what to make of it. "You good? How's Elmo?"

"Okay," the little boy sheepishly replies.

"Good, good. What's your name, buddy?"

The boy doesn't say anything, instead looking to his mother, a svelte sunken cheeked woman Bruce would probably hit with a pickup line under other circumstances.

"His name is Harper," she says, her voice wavering. "He has nightmares. We're just here to see the doctor."

"It's all good," Bruce assures her. "Harper, you like superheroes?"

Harper nods his head up and down after a queue of approval from his mother.

"Ok, buddy," Bruce says. "Me and my friends here are from Shield, and we're just here to find some bad guys. So you just sit tight and we'll be out of here in no time."

"Okay."

"Cute kid, lady," Bruce says.

Fleabag brings Dr. Sartorius in behind them, hands still zip tied and looking disheveled from being tackled by five large men. His mop of grey hair hangs in his face adding a wild aspect to his appearance that is probably unbefitting of the potbellied middle-aged doctor.

"Doctor!" screeches the secretary when she sees him.

"It's alright, Debbie," he assures her with impossible confidence. For all that guy knows they're going to shoot everybody here in the face and set the building on fire. "This is all just some kind of mix-up."

"Did you find anything deeper in?" Helen asks Fleabag.

The werewolf tilts his head with some uncertainty. "Some locked up crackpots, some not so locked up crackpots, a bunch of orderlies we rounded up in a side room. Not anything from the realm of science fiction. The prisoners have the serial code tattoos we're looking for though."

"Prisoners?" the doctor objects. "No one is a prisoner here."

"Alright. Cut the doctor loose," Helen orders. "But I'm warning you now, Sartorius. You go for any weapons and we will ventilate you."

"Like an HVAC technician," Fleabag menacingly assures, adding an awkward cap to a metaphor that already wasn't the greatest. He cuts the zip tie with a little pig sticker from a holster on his suspenders.

"We don't have any weapons," Sartorius says, wringing his hands after having them loosed. "What did they tell you we do here?"

"Nobody told us what you do here," Helen answers. "Nobody told us there was a here at all."

"One of your sideshow freaks is on a killing spree south of the border," Bruce says.

"Mexico?" Sartorius pats down his unruly hair.

"No, dope. The U.S."

"Oh, right. I'm originally from Texas. You never really get used to that whole northern southern thing. It doesn't feel like a different country up here. I think it's because the language doesn't change. Everyone is so much nicer here though, so there are those subtle things."

"Okay great," Helen cuts the doctor off. "Tell us about your human experiments."

"That's not how I would characterize what I do."

"No one ever does." Helen rolls her eyes.

"Do you want to meet some of the patients?" Sartorius says. "Come on back."

The group follows Sartorius through a set of double doors displaying a shiny silver placard which commands *Do Not Enter Without Desk Attendant's Approval*. Another identical set of doors immediately greets them at the other side of a very short blank hallway. "You probably scared some of these people half to death," the doctor says as he pushes his way into the next room. Fleabag sticks to him like glue, clogging the doorway. His eyes stay fixed on Sartorius like he's just barely holding back from making a lunch of the doctor.

Bruce steps into the next room and is again taken by surprise. It's a large open recreational room, the kind he would expect to see in an old folks home. There are some couches surrounding a large patterned rug on the white tile floor and a television. A dumpy man in a bathrobe is playing solitaire on a flimsy looking card table and a frail woman on one of the couches is writing on a spiral bound notepad in complete ignorance of the television nearby.

"This looks like the place where we put my mother-in-law," Helen says.

"Our clinic is a lot like what you might encounter at an assisted living community, with certain important differences, of course." Sartorius moves to the man at the card table and gently nudges his shoulder. "Randy? Randy? Cyan, two, nine, three, blue."

Randy springs to life as if a loud noise just awakened him from a grain-alcohol induced coma. "Huh-huh?" His eyes dart around the room, taking in the presence of the commandos. "Oh, there are people here."

"Randy, we have some unexpected visitors and some of the others might be scared. Can you go around and tell everyone that everything is okay?"

"Yeah." Randy nods way too affirmatively. His eyes refuse to focus on anything at all. "I won't let you down, doc." He stands up from the table and pushes in his chair before hurrying off through a finished woodgrain door to some other part of the building. The door is too homey looking for a hospital. Most of the decor here is warm in that way. The couches appear newer and the walls are painted with a leafy print instead of the sterile white of some death clinic.

Bruce looks over the shoulder of the woman on the couch, down into her lap, where her boney hands move across lines of notebook paper, recording a long list of what appear to be serial or model numbers, because they include letters with the numbers.

"You working on a project there?" he asks, but she never looks up or acknowledges his presence. Bruce notes the tattoo on the underside of her forearm, which reads *Burgundy 1 1 7 Red*.

"Doris never speaks, and we're not certain she can hear you either. We bring her around to use the bathroom every few hours and that's it."

"What's she doing with the notepad?" Bruce asks, following along as Doris writes another long alphanumeric on the next line of paper.

"She's trainspotting."

"Where?" Helen asks.

The doctor throws his hands up. "Who knows?"

# INT. F4PL0RD'S APARTMENT - DAY

F4pl0rd's building is in Lincoln Park. It is well-lit and well-kept, and there is an elevator which Sid refuses to take. After a very brief disagreement about that, Jamie ends up explaining about F4pl0rd on the way up the stairs.

"He's a literal Nazi," Jamie rasps, on the third flight of stairs. "He's conducted raids, abuse, targeted harassment campaigns. He's a rapist. He's the worst kind of scum there is."

"Why hasn't anyone killed him?"

"We can't just kill him."

"He's that powerful?"

"It's complicated."

"How do you know him?"

"He initiated a mass rape attack on SparklyLips87, the Twitch streamer, that went on for days. Hundreds of trolls were involved. They were using sock puppets. There was nothing anybody could do to stop it. We tried de-platforming, and I doxxed him, which is why I know where he lives, but nothing worked. He still has seven hundred thousand followers."

Apparently, in addition to his computer hacking skills, this F4pl0rd is a formidable warlord with a vicious penchant for sexual atrocities. Sid is uncertain whether that makes him more or less relatable.

Jamie points out F4pl0rd's apartment door quietly when they reach the seventh floor of the building and Sid notes the unusual bright yellow doormat placed below the peephole, which features an S shaped squiggle of black marker intended to depict a snake, but clearly drawn by a small talentless child or invalid. Below the squiggle is a warning: *No step on snek.*

He knocks on the door, steps to the side, and waits beside the door frame. He never waits in front of a door, especially if it has a peephole. The space immediately outside a door is the death zone, where all the bullets will go if somebody inside decides to shoot through the relatively flimsy wood paneling with a fully automatic rifle. Sid never stands in the death zone.

He holds up a finger to shush Jamie as they wait. After a few moments of silence, he hears a slight creak from the other side, probably the hacker or one of his soldiers checking the peephole. Sid waits for an additional fifteen seconds, then knocks again from beside the door. A moment later, the opening of the door is first announced by the sliding of a chain bolt and deadbolt. The picosecond the knob turns, Sid whips around the jamb and forces his way inside the apartment with an FNX pistol shoved into the teeth of whomever happened to be looking outside.

The apartment is hardly what Sid expected from a vicious thug of the caliber Jamie described. The walls are covered by dozens of colorful anime posters, most of them sporting giant-eyed, scantily clad, impossibly huge breasted, impossibly tiny-waisted, caricatures of human females with unnaturally bright colors of hair. Come to think of it, they all look a lot like Mary Sue.

F4pl0rd screams something that becomes incomprehensible as Sid jams the barrel of the FNX into the hacker's mouth. Sid forces the pudgy man backward over the arm of a lint laden couch, and then leans to look down an adjoining hallway for additional threats. The hallway is empty except for a few open doorways.

"Make any noise and I blow your fucking brains out," Sid growls. "Who else is here with you?" He pulls the FNX suppressor from F4pl0rd's mouth so the hacker can answer. F4pl0rd dry-heaves loudly as Sid presses a combat boot down on his pot belly, just below a worn image of a green cartoon frog with bright red lips.

"No-nobody," Ptrkpt sputters. "Who are you?"

"I am death incarnate. You are boot scum. You are also lying. Where are your sentries, warlord?"

"What? What are you talking about? Wh-" F4pl0rd sees Jamie enter the apartment behind Sid and his revulsion is both spontaneous and severe. "You! What the fuck are you doing here?!"

Jamie winces in equal parts disgust and embarrassment. "I really don't think all of this is necessary, Sid."

Sid applies some further scrutiny to his surroundings, which include a display of cheap ornamental Japanese swords, numerous painted statues of anime characters, and a five foot tall pillow featuring a life-size print of a purple-haired anime girl with goat horns spreading her dripping cartoon labia wide open in lascivious anticipation. No pillaging badass would ever desire to own such a pathetic artifact of sexual desperation. Sid's own self-styled rape god of a brother would have cackled about that pillow all the way through brutally ravaging the next suitable female he encountered.

"This guy isn't actually a warlord, is he?" Sid questions, looking back incredulously to Jamie.

"Not exactly," Jamie wavers. "I think we've had a miscommunication."

"You said he led an army that raped some girl to death with sock puppets and made thousands of people watch."

"You fucking third wave feminazi cunts!" F4pl0rd shrieks. "Everything is rape with you idiots!"

"Rape culture is real, douchebag," Jamie fires back.

Sid wipes hacker drool from the FNX suppressor onto the weird anime sex girl pillow and then holsters the gun.

"Did you just SWAT me because I made fun of some retard online?" F4pl0rd calls out. "Is that what this is about?"

"No! This has nothing to do with that!"

"You're fucking crazy! I'm calling the cops!"

"You're not calling the cops," Sid assures him. "Just calm down. We came here because I need a computer hacker and you're the only one Jamie knows."

"That stupid trap doesn't know me! I almost lost everything because it got me suspended from Twitter!"

"For making rape threats!" Jamie says.

"All I said was she could turn the game off if she didn't like it!"

"That's victim blaming!"

"She had more views on that stream than she ever had before! She got ten grand in donations overnight! She was loving it!"

"She was crying and telling you to stop!"

"Are you two talking about a video game? Is that what's happening here?"

"Yeah. SparklyLips87 did a stream for *Call of Honor: Comfort Battalion* and she was terribad at it, like she couldn't even strafe and turn at the same time, so I posted a link on 4chan and we raided her server with avatars that all looked like Staff Sergeant Lincoln Osiris and everybody did hump emotes on top of her character while spamming 'Never go full retard' and she started crying. It was funny, so we just kept doing it."

"It was sexual violence!" Jamie shrieks.

"That's not violence," Sid says. "No bodies. No violence."

"Thank you! That's what these SJW nitwits can't get through their heads. Now get the fuck out of my apartment!"

"No. I need you to do some hacking for me or there's going to be violence. The real kind."

"Hacking? I don't know anything about hacking."

"You're full of it," Jamie squeaks. "I know you defaced Renita Snarcheesian's site."

"I had nothing to do with that, but whoever was responsible is an unparalleled genius."

"Violence. Real violence." Sid whips the FNX back out of its holster and pokes the muzzle into F4pl0rd's forehead to remind him of the very tangible threat he poses.

"Okay, I may have some modest Javascript experience."

"I have an IP address. I need to know who it belongs to."

"The best computer hacker in the world could only get you a physical address. No guarantees about who actually used it to do whatever it is you guys are angry about. If it's a public terminal like a library or a cyber cafe or something it could have been anybody."

"Just get me a street number and I'll find the fucker from there."

"Damn. What did this guy do?"

"He framed BuzzWorthy for building an evil supercomputer and now a ghost monster is trying to kill Jamie."

"I see." The blank look in the hacker's eyes indicates that Sid's explanation was either maddening or inadequate, but he doesn't care to explain things any further. He's been through it too many times already today.

"I don't have time for this," Sid grumbles, writing the IP address on a Burger King bag he found on the floor near the couch. He tears the scrap with the number from the bag and holds it out to F4pl0rd. "Get hacking."

# INT. THE VEIDT INSTITUTE - DAY

Dr. Sartorius pours himself some tea from a pot on a hot plate in a tiny little side room adjoining the recreational area. In following him through a few rooms at the facility, Bruce has learned that the man is unusually friendly and also unusually long winded, but in an especially obnoxious way in which most of his ideas are expressed in a series of fast moving run-on sentences interrupted by other run-on sentences.

"Are you sure you don't want any? It's Earl Grey. I find tea keeps me sharp through the day, but doesn't keep me up all night like coffee, so I made the switch. You really need to strike that balance."

"No thanks," Helen turns down the tea. Bruce has never been a tea man either.

"The tattoos all the patients got," Bruce says. "We thought that shit was a serial number, but that ain't it, is it?"

"A serial number?" Sartorius says. "Good lord, no. That would be dehumanizing. Those are medical tattoos. They're intended for emergencies really, but we use them pretty casually around the clinic."

"That's not like any medical tattoo I've ever seen," Fleabag says.

"How many medical tattoos have you seen?" Bruce comments.

"I was in the corps. Some guys get their blood type, chronic conditions. Not this James Bond spy code stuff."

"Hmmm," Sartorius purses his lips. "I never really thought about how it looks to someone without any context. I guess you do have a point."

"You read back the tattoo and whatshisface popped right out of his trance," Bruce observes.

"Correct. One of the first things we do with new patients is assign them a passphrase which we can use as a trigger to bring them out of any remote experience. We condition the phrases through a series of hypnotic suggestions and the phrases are then inscribed directly on the patients for quick reference in case of emergency."

"Emergency? You mean in case one of them sees something they're not supposed to?"

"More like if their physical body is in immediate danger. Not all of the patients are as calm as Randy and Doris. Sometimes we have to restrain them to keep them from hurting themselves." Sartorius pauses for some consideration, then adds "Or others."

"So that's all this place is? A big nursing home for remote viewers?" Helen asks.

"Not entirely. I'm not thrilled with the connotations of the nursing home term. I mean around here we call it the n-word, you know? I mean it's not THE n-word, but it's the other n-word. No offense." Sartorius directs his justification at Bruce, who blanks for a second, unsure if anything the doctor said could actually be construed by anyone as offensive.

"None taken?" Bruce says.

"These people with these abilities, past even a minimal level, they need round the clock care. I saw it when I was working with the British government—

across the pond, as they like to say—and after that project ended I came to R&D and I said 'guys, we have a unique opportunity here.' It comes together perfectly. We provide necessary medical care, easily beyond the quality of what any of these viewers would receive in a more conventional setting—I think we can all agree on that—most of these manifestations would be dismissed as symptoms of schizophrenia or dementia in any other mental health facility for Christ's sake. So we take care of them, free of charge to families and healthcare providers, thanks to your generous benefactors, and while they're here we get to . . . observe."

"What are you observing?"

"Fascinating things, Mr. Freeman. Absolutely fascinating things."

"You ever observe anybody turn into a evil looking ghost monster that walks through walls and pushes people out windows?"

"Excuse me?"

"What Mr. Freeman is trying to ask is if you've seen anything beyond expectation here at the facility. Can any of the viewers do more than just view?"

"You mean telekinesis?"

"Anything at all."

"No. Never. But I should tell you we can't see what they see. We rely on the viewers' accounts for data, and those accounts are very often unreliable. So many of the patients experience severe psychosis."

"Why do they all go crazy, doctor?"

"That's one of the few aspects of the condition we do understand. They're lost in what they see, even when they come back. It has a profound effect."

"What's that supposed to mean? Can't they just pull it together?"

"That's easy for you to say, but imagine if your entire life was like a series of dreams, and you kept waking up from one into another, never sure if you were waking up in the real world or a facsimile. Eventually you would forget whole dreams and with them whole worlds. It's a little bit like that, but even worse. The stronger viewers aren't anchored by their place in the physical world. They're almost constantly adrift, out there somewhere, looking at people and places far away. When we try to communicate with them it only confuses them. We might sound like a voice in their head if they can hear us at all. A number of them don't seem to have any concept of where their real body is located even when they do briefly return to it. Others don't return at all, or live in a juxtaposed state, seeing two places at once, alternating, seeing one and hearing another, or any combination of those things."

"What about the patient who assassinated a regional council candidate last year here in Toronto? He was one of the more disturbed viewers, I'm guessing?"

"Alex Hinter, and no, actually. We were treating him for relatively limited manifestations. When he told me he had viewed that politician initiating a nuclear war in the future, I dismissed it as a probable nightmare or psychotic episode, but now I'm not so sure."

"Wait. Are you implying that some of them can see into the future?"

"Well, no. Although I wouldn't rule it out as a possibility. I am very probably the world's foremost expert on this phenomenon, and I'll be the first to tell you we do not have the foggiest notion what makes it work or what limits it may reach."

"When we landed here, you already knew we were coming. You said you were expecting us."

"That's a parlor trick, not time-travel. I only needed to know you were on your way to know that you would be arriving."

"And who told you we were on our way?"

"That would be our most gifted patient. Would you two like to meet the somnambulist?"

# INT. F4PL0RD'S APARTMENT - DAY

Sid stands in the messy rear bedroom of F4pl0rd's apartment while the hacker clicks through a series of digital boxes and other computerized doodads with Jamie gazing suspiciously over his shoulder. The room looks like a fast food garbage dump, with rolled up bags from a half dozen different burger joints strewn around F4pl0rd's keyboard and a hip-high stack of pizza boxes in one corner that Sid estimates must be weeks old for the simple fact that no human could ingest that much pizza in a shorter span. None of this interests him though. The object of his attention is a green and white nylon flag that takes up most of a wall opposite the computer setup. The flag is an image of a black cross with a white circle at its intersection, framing a stylized logo that looks like the letters KEK written both horizontally and vertically, and with each K inverted so the design can be read right to left or left to right.

"What is this thing?" Sid asks.

"It's the KEK flag," F4pl0rd answers. "The flag of the Nation of Kekistan."

"Where is that? It sounds like the Middle East, but I've been there, and it's not there."

"We are a disparate and dispossessed people."

"It doesn't exist," Jamie scoffs. "It's a made up country for miscreants and racists."

"Kind of like a made up gender for deviants who want to use the wrong bathroom?" F4pl0rd says.

"I'm not a deviant."

"Do any of you people do anything real?" Sid asks. "Or are your whole lives bullshit? I mean you're pretending you're some kind of non-human he/she. He's from a made-up country that fake rapes cartoon girls in video games. More stuff you made up on the internet put you in the crosshairs of a guy who imagines himself into existing. What the fuck? Seriously, what the fuck? What's wrong with all of you?"

"Fuck that," F4pl0rd says. "I'm all about not believing in any of that made-up Cultural Marxist trash."

"Here he goes with the snarl words," Jamie says.

"It's not a snarl word," F4pl0rd snarls. "It's the truth. This brand of Frankfort School politically correct postmodern nonsense is destroying western civilization. You can't even say normal words anymore without worrying about a Twitter lynch mob going after your job or some blue haired gender studies grad calling you a white nationalist in a think piece that gets four thousand shares before lunch break."

"Please. Your toxic brand of paleoconservative late capitalism is the only thing destroying the country. You people had the mic for two centuries and now CEOs make two hundred seventy one times as much as most workers. Millennials with college degrees can't even find work above minimum wage service jobs."

"It's not our fault you retards get college degrees in holistic music therapy. I'm a millennial. I went to trade school for CS and I've got a downright cushy gig."

"Because you're a white cis male."

"So are you!"

"That's misgendering."

"You have a dick."

"How sure are you about that?" Sid interjects. "Like on a one to ten scale?"

"At least a six," F4pl0rd replies, not sounding all too certain himself.

"You're a transphobic racist piece of shit!" Jamie says.

"Here we go with the phobias and the isms. Everybody's a sexist racist transphobic homophobic because they don't agree with your talking points."

"Your whole subculture is based on racist frog memes and cyberbullying people who aren't like you!"

"At least it's funny! Your whole subculture is based on inventing new ways to be victimized so you can blame us for it!"

"Inventing? Did we invent Nazi Pepe? Or tits or GTFO? Or dindu nuffins? Or We Wuz Kangz an Shiet?"

"No. Cause left can't meme. Besides, we only do that stuff because you fuckers tell us we can't. We don't actually mean it."

"You still say it. If you say it, you mean it!"

"Fuck that! I say a whole lot of stuff I don't mean. It's just for the lols!"

"Hate speech and bigotry are never funny!"

"Fuck that! They're funny at least half the time!"

"Do you hear this?" Jamie says, looking to Sid in provocation.

"I think you both sound stupid," Sid says. "We're not getting anywhere with the IP address either."

"I already tracked it back to AT&T," F4pl0rd says.

"Really? I thought there would be more typing or something."

"This isn't TV." F4pl0rd pulls a cheap cell phone and another boxy electronic gadget Sid cannot identify from a drawer under his mousepad. "It'll take a little while to get an address." He begins dialing.

"What are you doing? Ordering a pizza?" Sid says.

"No. I'm hacking the ISP."

"But you do that on the computer. . ."

"You do part of it on the computer. Most of it is old fashioned legwork. I set up a malware app on an FTP with a landing page. I'm spoofing my number so it looks like I'm calling from inside the company. Now I call tech support and work my magic."

"Huh?"

F4pl0rd's magic is truly impressive. He responds with a tired sounding monotone as someone picks up his call. "Hi, Winston. Pat from marketing. I'm working on that thing for Mr. Kennard." He's pulling names from a chart on his desktop monitor which he acquired while he and Jamie were arguing. "I can't get this thing he linked to me to open. He's gonna be pissed if this isn't done before his three o'clock. Can you tell me what the problem is?"

Sid and Jamie watch in silence as F4pl0rd talks his way through this transaction in a completely different persona than the one they met when Sid kicked the door in. It's as if, for these few minutes, he is no longer a fat slob with a neckbeard half-buried in Doritos bags and weeb toys, but a smooth talking high level exec— the kind of guy who sells ketchup popsicles to Eskimos wearing white gloves, the kind of guy Sid absolutely cannot stand. They watch and listen as F4pl0rd calls the VP of the company a 'real pain in the left nut' and proceeds to direct the nameless peon from the tech support line to navigate to a web page he provides and click a link found there. "Oh? It's working now? Maybe it was just my connection. I'm on a hotspot. Who knows? Thanks. How late will you be here today? Ok, cool. I'll call back before then if I need anything." And then F4pl0rd disconnects the call.

"What was that?" Sid says.

"That was me getting some guy in the basement of the AT&T building in Dallas to click a link that installs my remote desktop software on his work machine."

"And that tells us where the IP is?"

"No. That lets us restart his computer."

"Why do we want to do that?"

"Because he'll have to log back in after it reboots and now we have a key logger on the system, so we get his username and password that way."

"So now we just log in and get the address ourselves."

"No. Now we watch TV until five o'clock when Winston goes home."

"Why can't we just do it now?"

"Because they'll realize they've been hacked when they see the computer moving around. Pro-tip: Always call a domestic department for this shit. Americans go home at five, but hajji never sleeps."

"See what I'm talking about?" Jamie says. "Racist."

"He makes some compelling points," Sid says.

# INT. THE VEIDT INSTITUTE - DAY

The patient Dr. Sartorius refers to as the somnambulist resides somewhere behind a keycard door in the basement of the facility. Bruce would hardly call it high level security, as anybody with a handgun could probably take this whole place alone and shoot the bolts out of the door. Most of the locks in this place are here to keep the patients from moving between rooms, not to keep soldiers out.

"We've been conducting some trials of a synthetic formula designed by myself and Doctor Gorsky for a few months now," Sartorius says. "The objective is to see if we can stabilize some of the more unruly patients, though focusing the viewing ability seems to be an incidental little bonus. In tests, it appears that anchoring the viewers gives them more control over what they see. They can focus better. The results are mixed overall, but Max has shown marked improvements since taking the formula. A few months ago he was in a permanently comatose state. Now he's communicative beyond anything Stargate ever hoped for."

The doctor slides his keycard through the reader next to the door and waits for the little red LED indicator to alternate to green. Then he leads Helen and Bruce through the doors into a quiet little room which is well lit, despite any eerie vibes previously conjured by Sartorius's eerie description of its occupant. Other attributes are all quite sterile. The walls and floor are white. There are no decorations or personal effects. There are only two objects inside: a hospital bed and a stainless steel box which Bruce identifies as either a large freezer, or a coffin, or maybe something in-between. Bruce wonders if it is full of explosives, or if some kind of evil thing is hiding for them inside. He keeps waiting for the other shoe to drop in the form of a death trap or a laboratory full of sick human experiments, but so far they just keep being wrong about this Sartorius guy.

"He needs this sensory deprivation tank to focus the visions now," Sartorius says. "But he comes up once in a while so we can have a chat." The doctor draws a small bottle of darkly colored liquid from a rack attached to the rail of the hospital bed. He inserts a syringe into the top of the bottle, carefully filling it to a measured dosage. "Max is the most capable remote viewer we've ever encountered. I think that goes for all of the other programs too, Russians included. With our current course of treatments he's getting even stronger."

"How long ago did you start the treatments?" Helen asks.

"About six weeks. Why?"

Helen's gaze shifts communicatively to Bruce. The timing matches up perfectly with the start of the blogger murders.

Sartorius raps on the side of the drum not too loudly. Bruce prepares to draw his gun just in case, though nothing happens immediately. A moment later Sartorius knocks again and opens the blank lid. Inside, the somnambulist rests in a bath of clear salt water.

"Max," Sartorius says. "You have some visitors."

The somnambulist does not move. His expression never changes. He does not speak a word. He floats at the surface of the water, still as a corpse, the whole scene conjuring the discovery of some ancient mummy in its sarcophagus. His skin glistens from the water that fills the tank. His face is clean shaven and his flesh is smooth. If this is the transient, he looks a lot cleaner than the monster they've been fighting for the last twenty four hours.

Sartorius presses down on the syringe plunger, emptying the needle of air, and squirting a thin stream of formula into the air before lowering the needle to the sleeper's arm. "We hope that the formula will lead to a major breakthrough in treatment at the very least, and possibly even some progress toward harnessing the viewing ability, but we're limited by the components in the current synthesis. In larger doses it is quite toxic." Sartorius carefully injects the sleeper with the formula. With no other sign of motion, the somnambulist's eyelids raise and his dark eyes shift over to Bruce and stay. Bruce feels unsettled quite quickly, as though the sleeping man's gaze is a ray of anxiety. It won't stop him from what he needs to do.

"The code on his arm," Helen says, stepping closer to get a good look down into the tank over Bruce's shoulder. "We need to see it." The medical tattoo is currently obstructed, as the somnambulist's arm rests against his body, hands folded over the tight pair of underwear which is his only clothing.

Sartorius gives the others a puzzled glance, then reaches slowly into the tank to lift up the somnambulist's wrist so they can read the fading black lettering.

Drab 4 6 8 Grey.

"It's not him," Bruce says.

"It has to be somebody else in the facility then," Helen mutters. "Dr. Sartorius, how many of your patients don't stay here at the center?"

"Very few," Sartorius answers, suddenly gaining a leery tone which Bruce would judge to be uncharacteristic from what he has seen of the man. "What exactly is this about? What are you two looking for?"

Helen gives pause before answering, but whatever she opens her mouth to say is interrupted by the raspy voice from within the deprivation tank beside them.

"You'll find only anguish here," the somnambulist says. "The thing you seek has not become."

"The hell does that mean?" Bruce says.

"The divergent path circles back to its own crossroad."

"What's he talking about?"

Sartorius is without a guess. "I don't know. He's usually much more concise."

"I see the evil thing in two of its places now, Bruce Freeman. Fear, horror. It knows I am watching. It does not care."

"How do we stop it?" Helen says.

"Kill. No other way."

"Kill it how? We need to know how."

"You already know. It is unfortunate."

"I don't like that. What do you think that means?" Bruce says. Helen doesn't spend much time brooding over an answer.

"Maybe nothing. We need to find Fleabag and see if he found anything. This is a waste of our time," Helen says, heading for the door. Bruce sticks with her.

"What are you looking for?" Sartorius asks again, as he disposes of his needle in a plastic biohazardous waste bin with a big warning sticker on the side.

"I told you before, doc," Bruce reiterates with some annoyance. "A remote viewer that shows up looking like a zombie and gets into people's heads, flies, walks through walls, does whatever he wants."

"That's absurd. Not even Max can do those things."

"Well, this thing can. Okay, doc?" Bruce snarks back at the doctor forcefully. "I've seen it. Been chasing it around since yesterday. People are dead now. And it has one of your medical code tattoos. You care to explain that?"

"I can't."

"You got to, because we got to find this guy and waste him before he kills again."

"Waste him?"

"How many other patients have been administered the formula since you started?" Helen cuts in, before Bruce has to explicitly define that euphemism for a grown man who should know damn well what he means.

"Only six. What's the code you're looking for?"

"Aqua six one six green," Helen informs the doctor slowly to avoid any mistake in the numbers.

"It's not one I know," Sartorius says. "I'll have to look it up."

"Let's do that," Bruce suggests. The doctor shuts the somnambulist back in his tank and then Bruce and Helen follow him back through the sets of security doors toward the front of the facility. They find Fleabag back in the rec room where they first split up and he offers them only disappointing news.

"We made the rounds of the whole place," Fleabag says. "All three floors. None of the patients has that tattoo."

"That isn't possible," Sartorius insists. "Not unless it's one of the outpatients, but they manifest very minimally."

"Somebody could'a been hiding under a bed or something, but I doubt it." The werewolf pokes the tip of his nose. "You can't hide from the old sniffer."

Back in the waiting room at the front of the facility, Sartorius quietly asks Debbie the receptionist to help him look up the transient's code in their computer system. Bruce and Helen are waiting at the reception desk when Sartorius looks at the computer screen and turns the color of paste. His difficulty in offering up an explanation for what he sees is palpable.

"What?" Helen goads, as she and Bruce both wait for the doctor to tell them anything at all. "Who is it?"

"It's . . . uh. . ." Sartorius trails off. "It's not in there." He's a terrible liar.

"What do you mean it's not in there?" Helen rises up threateningly—something she doesn't do often. "Does Fleabag need to help you put it back in there?" The werewolf closes in, walking behind the reception desk eagerly.

Bruce is watching Sartorius's eyes. He has been for a minute now. He saw them move from the computer, to Helen, then somewhere across the room, then back down to settle on the keyboard as if the meaning of life was written across the space bar. This is a dead give-away. When people look at something and they don't want others to think they looked at it, they always avert their eyes to something insignificant, something they pick at random upon the revelation they are being watched. That's why Bruce doesn't need the doctor to answer any more questions.

"Helen," Bruce nudges the Graveyard director's elbow as she relatively discreetly grumbles veiled and not-so-veiled threats at the doctor.

"I don't think you want this guy beating answers out of you. . ."

"Helen," Bruce repeats.

"What?"

"There." Bruce points to the other side of the waiting room where little Harper plays with a color coded bead maze next to his worried mother and a much more lax Graveyard operator. The little code on the underside of the boy's wrist is plainly visible.

Aqua 6 1 6 Green

# INT. THE CATACOMBS - DAY

**SUPER: The Distant Future**

Harper climbs from the hulking stainless steel drum on the plastic rungs of a rope ladder Colonel Green hung into the salt solution. The tingling in his hands is the precursor to the burning he will feel when sensation returns to them. He already itches everywhere else, and when the painkillers wear off it will be far worse. He doesn't care. He slams his clenched fist down on the lip of the container where Green stands on an iron riser waiting with a ragged beach towel to collect him. The faded markings Aqua 6 1 6 Green, put there at the Veidt institute decades ago, are beginning to flake from his wrist altogether.

"This can't be!" he screams. "I did it! How is it this nightmare remains unchanged?!"

"Did it? Did what?" the colonel questions. "The files still read the same way. We probably wouldn't know if they changed though. . ."

"The files say I killed Chan?"

"No. Sid Hansen stopped you. That's what they said before you went back, right?"

"I have to go back again!" Harper bellows, ooze leaking across his right eye from the flesh sloughing above his brow. "I must have doubled up, gone back too far ahead. This is why Hansen was so confused in the park. Shoot me up and put me back in the tank."

"You're out of your mind!" the colonel barks as Harper brushes the towel aside. "You look like Hell! You won't last another jump back!"

"It doesn't matter, Allen! None of it matters unless I erase the whole list!"

"Your face is going to fall off before you do that!"

"You think I care about that?! If I can fix what happened, if there's even a chance, then I'm going out fixing it!"

"Ryan says he's not even sure Wyatt is one of the bloggers anymore!"

"That's wrong! It has to be one of them!"

"There are pieces that don't match up in Anderson's reports. It never says anything about what happened to Chan after Chicago. If Chan was really Wyatt, don't you think they would say something?"

"He could have gagged them somehow. You know how that freak does things!" Harper shouts, climbing from the tank as a char-grey husk of cracked flesh and wild white hair. The irony of him calling anyone a freak is not lost on him. "If nobody can kill him back then, they probably can't talk about him either!"

"We don't know that." Colonel Green follows Harper down the ladder from the riser, pacing himself to stay clear of Harper's fingers in an overly cautious way that bothers Harper-makes him feel weak.

The nurse—Harper doesn't know her name even though she is the only nurse who works with him—comes over to check his vitals as he rasps, struggling to stand on the cold concrete floor.

"I can't believe you're still moving," she says. "Your blood pressure is shit. Colonel, his condition is critical."

"I'm fine," Harper insist.

"That's the drugs talking."

"They're not loud enough. Give me more."

"You're already so full of steroids and painkillers it's a miracle you can stand."

"I don't care! I already killed Chan! I saw it happen, but I have to go back again to make it come out right! It must be why this place is still . . . this place. I still have to go back and help myself."

"You're delirious."

"No. It's too complicated to explain right now. Once it's done, the alteration of the timeline will be complete. I have to go back and stop Sid Hansen from stopping me."

"We already know he stops you!" Colonel Green tries to reason, but his appeal is deeply flawed.

"Then send me back and make him stop me! If we sit here and do nothing we get the same result! We get that!" Harper points to a monitor bank far over the nurse's shoulder, though she doesn't follow his aim back to it. She never looks at it. Neither does the colonel. If they did, they would be angry like Harper—angry enough to do something. If they could see it the way he sees, they would be even angrier.

The monitor displays the top-down feed of the Las Vegas strip taken from the gargantuan spy satellite Vedrfolnir. The strip ceased to be a site of revelry long ago, at least in any conventional sense. The hordes had gathered there after most of the other cities were cleansed by nuclear fire after the Deconstruction. Most of those died out in time, unable to plan beyond immediate desires for shiny things and whatever food was convenient. Now the strip is a field of concrete and rotting skeletons that stretches for miles. Some starved, but most fell to violence spurred by hunger, sexual conquest, or just whimsy-the Frankies will happily kill each other for no other reason than they feel like it. A lone living figure hovers over a wilted corpse at the edge of the Bellagio's sprawling fountain, probably having sex with it, because that's the kind of thing they do. Harper has seen that and so much worse. The others can only look down on it all from above, but he can float freely through the disaster areas and corpse piles. The Frankies certainly don't bother to bury the dead. Some wash themselves out of vanity, but none clean or maintain anything around them. The uncleansed areas have become stinking cesspools rife with horrors. Harper has seen entire piles of bodies that died mid-orgy, with putrefied mooshy centers, and an outer crust of late comers still not quite stiff with rigor mortis. He has seen a solid gold toilet piled with feces since the water stopped working. He has seen them eat each other and themselves. He has seen the smoking fusion of flesh and fiberglass left behind when a Bugatti Veyron slams into the Washington Monument at four-hundred miles per hour.

"If you two won't help me, I'll do it myself!"

"He'll kill you!" the colonel says. "We already know that happens!"

"I'm dead anyway!" This is only a slight hyperbole. Sartorious died long before he could doing anything to lessen the toxicity of the chemical cocktail he used to treat the remote viewers in his care. The massive dosages Harper takes to permit manipulation of past events have taken their toll over the last forty-eight hours. Previously, the massive tumor in his brain was killing him slowly. Now the chemicals are killing him quickly. "What difference does it make?"

The nurse looks like she wants to say something, but she doesn't. Neither does Green. Neither of them are moving fast enough for Harper's taste.

"Where are the drugs?" he demands. "Just give me the bottle. I'll shoot it up myself." Harper shambles for the cabinet where he knows they keep the steroids, but more importantly, the cocktail that allows him to focus his remarkable sight-focus it with such intensity that he no longer simply sees a faraway place, but personifies himself there. He stumbles only a few feet into his trip. He's falling apart fast, but not fast enough to keep him from one last daydream.

Defeated by his obstinance, the nurse steps ahead of him. "Here," she offers, seemingly unable to look him in the eyes. She takes a bottle from the racks of pills, vials, and other medical appliances.

"Give me all of it!" Harper commands. Sid Hansen won't stop him this time. No one will stop him this time.

## INT. THE VEIDT INSTITUTE - DAY

SUPER: Present Day

Fleabag hauls Sartorius through the white hallway trailing Bruce and Helen. His eyes become wild bloodshot things, veiny and narrow as he whips the doctor through the doors into the rec room like nothing more than a child's doll.

"You're not really going to do this!" Sartorius shouts. "That's a child for Christ's sake!" Fleabag slaps a hairy hand over the doctor's mouth to shut him up.

"This can't really be happening," Bruce says. He should probably not be surprised, all things considered, but this last development has exceeded even his stretched expectations. "How is it even possible?"

Helen doesn't look any less shocked. "Mary Sue said the viewer isn't from now," she says. "We thought she was hysterical, but she was making perfect sense. He came here from the future."

"No shit!" Bruce yells.

"What are we supposed to do now?" Fleabag wants to know. "Build a time machine and go shoot the fucker in twenty-ninety-two or whatever year he's from?"

"We don't need a time machine. I mean, he's right here," Bruce says.

"He's not right here. That's the baby transient," Fleabag says. "We need to kill the grown-up transient."

"It's the same thing. You kill him now, in his past, you kill him in the future. You never seen *Back to the Future*?"

"Is that the one with the guy from Teen Wolf?"

"I should have known," Bruce sighs. "Go do it, I guess."

"Do what?"

"Kill the kid."

"I'm not killing a kid! What the fuck!?"

"Nigga, you eat people!"

"Not kids."

"Pretend it's Little Red Riding Hood. Whatever you got to do."

"Nope. I didn't sign up for that."

"Yeah you did. You're in the number one official black helicopter black ops off the record deny everything outfit there is. That's exactly what you signed up for."

"No it's not," Helen says.

"See!" Bruce starts to reiterate. "That's an orde— hold up. That's not an order?"

"How are you so sure killing him now will even work?" Helen asks.

"It's not that complicated. We kill him now, he won't even exist later."

"Then he'll never come back here at all, so then we'll never have a reason to kill him, so we won't kill him. Grandfather paradox."

"So just cause he's back here is proof that we won't kill the kid."

"I guess. I don't know what will happen if we try."

"Why do we have to kill him?" Fleabag says. "What if you put him in protective custody? He's just a kid. We can give him a bunch of stuffed animals and get some babysitters and whatnot and just make sure he doesn't grow up to turn into that thing."

Helen doesn't respond. She already sees the same gap in that logic that Bruce sees.

"That could be exactly what we did to turn him into that thing," Bruce says.

"He's right," Helen agrees.

"Oh." Realization strikes the werewolf. "This is a serious mindfuck."

# INT. F4PL0RD'S APARTMENT - DAY

F4pl0rd sips from a can of cold and electrifyingly awesome Mountain Dew before finishing a story. "So then he says 'Maybe if you hit the treadmill a little more, you would be.'"

Sid cackles wildly. "That's hilarious!"

"Oh yeah. It's the best. You have to hear about the time some cuck tried to sue Dick for four hundred million dollars just because Dick banged his girlfriend."

"Was she hot?"

"Oh yeah. Dick only bangs the hottest chicks."

"I should find this Dick Masterson and learn from him."

Jamie sighs in overstated discontent from a beanbag chair in the corner of the messy room. "Are you ever going to actually hack the thing we need hacked or are we just going to sit here all day sharing sexist jokes?"

Sid shrugs. "I'm fine with either."

"Chill out, snowflake," F4pl0rd says, nudging his 18-button mouse to dismiss the screensaver rotating on the monitor in front of him.

"Yes, snowflake," says the transient. "Chill out."

Sid slings an FNX from its holster toward the source of the voice with lightning quickness. The transient stands embedded in the drywall, halfway between this room and the hallway outside. Sid looks down the pistol slide at the wreath of black flame obtenebrating the creature's head. The luminescent tritium night sights appear more like eyes than any feature of the transient's real face.

Jamie rushes for the door, but it slams shut, seemingly of its own volition. Jamie wraps both hands around the knob and pulls wildly to no avail.

"What do you plan to do with that, Sid?" the creature questions, staring down the barrel of Sid's gun. "Shoot me? You can't hurt me. I'm not even really here."

"I know that now. But I'm gonna find you where you really are, and I'm gonna turn your cranium into a glory hole."

"You and I will never meet. Not physically. Not in the same time. I already know that for certain. I know many things. I know where you will run when you finally get that door open. I know I'll kill Chan there. I've already been there. I've done it. You won't stop me. Do you understand how I know these things?"

"You can see the future."

"I'm from the future."

A bright flash illuminates the room, causing both Sid and the transient to glance at F4pl0rd, who is holding up a large Android cell phone to take a picture. "Sorry," the hacker says. "I need pics or /pol/ is never going to believe this."

"I come from two decades after the fall, when the first Frankies appeared, an America ravaged by nuclear war and roving degeneracy. The country is a wasteland, a kingdom of corpses. There are pockets of survivors the death cult hasn't found yet, but it won't be long before Mahdi hunts them down."

"What do you know about the Imam?" Sid knows about that sonofabitch, and he wishes he didn't. The old man thought the Imam was practically the devil in the flesh. Sid met the thing once, and it was the only fight he ever had in which he was indisputably outclassed. "You know how to kill him?"

"The 12th Imam, Harbinger of the End Times, Mahdi, Lord of the Death Cult. Yes. I can look upon his face as he sits on his imperial throne. He put it on top of the Freedom Tower. A tasteless choice, but not surprising given his proclivities. He is neither the architect of this horror or the true threat. Do you know what separates men from beasts, kill team? Self awareness? Consciousness? Souls? Those are all interpretations of the same thing. Language. Abstraction."

"I hate abstraction."

"You would. You're a notorious simpleton. If not, you might have stopped Wyatt when you had the chance. Instead, you let him strip away the only thing keeping our fragile society afloat. He reduced our language, and nearly all of the others, to nothing. He toppled Babel all over again while you chased your whores. As I told you when we first met, you stand for nothing. It disgusts me. But I'm here again to implore of you. Help me change the past."

"You've got it wrong," Sid says. "Jamie isn't Wyatt."

"You haven't any inkling of the raw power that madman wields—the foresight. I can tell you he expected these events already. He planned for them. He is playing with you. The Wyatt I know cannot be named or killed. We only call him Wyatt because his true name cannot be known."

"That's fucking crazy."

"No. He walks with your unwashed masses now, a secret king among the paupers. Those who see him do not remember his face if he does not wish it so. His weird magic is growing. Soon, no man will have the strength to harm him. I came back to kill him in this time, before he grows so strong."

"Seriously?" Sid remarks incredulously. He points at Jamie as the scrawny panicked waif rams the door in fruitless desperation—a flimsy door Sid could dash to splinters with a modest boot heel. "You really think that's the world destroyer?"

"We have the profiles generated by Comfort Eagle. Graveyard gave me Helen Anderson's personal reports."

"Graveyard gave them to you?"

"Well, future Graveyard." The transient tilts his flame blurred head. "Who do you think sent me back here to stop all this madness?"

"That's how you know where to find Jamie. It's not some fucking magic. You've just been reading Helen's files this whole time."

"Of course. That's how I knew only Chan survived my attempts, so Chan must have been Wyatt."

"Then why not just kill Chan? Why kill all of them?"

"The bloggers? I had to kill them to narrow it down to Chan. I just told you."

"But you said you already knew who it was before you started, because you read the files."

"Yes. Because I killed the others."

"But you didn't have to because you read the files."

"I don't understand. From my perspective, it simply is as it is. It may be there are other versions of the timeline where each of them or all of them lived, but I have no memory of those. I have no way to know what I already changed, or if it is at all possible to change the way any of this happened. I only know I keep returning to an apocalypse, and that I must keep trying."

"Is that a grandfather paradox?" F4pl0rd says.

"I don't know what that is," Sid grumbles. "Look man, you still have it wrong. There's another player involved. The real Wyatt built that codification mainframe for BuzzWorthy incognito. They never even met the guy."

"If I am wrong we have lost nothing but a sad creature that pitied its own confused existence. So what? What is the life of one aberrant against the lives of billions? You would risk that for this single homophile?"

"Some hero type would probably have a better answer to that question, but I'm just here for the whore money. That and after all this shit today I want to kill you just to prove I can."

"You are misguided," the transient says, floating gently from his place in the wall. As his body passes through the smudged white paint, Sid realizes that the creature had not been hovering at his level of the building. The wispy burning shadows emitted from the ghostly body obfuscated its proportions when only parts of it were poking through the drywall. Now the transient's upper half juts from the carpet in the open space of the room, his hips disappearing into the floor, but he remains eye-to-eye with the kill team.

He's huge. Just his torso is as tall as Sid. His legs are lost on some lower floor of the building.

Jamie won't stop screaming. F4pl0rd sits frozen in his chair, his cell phone remaining at the end of his outstretched arm, still as a statue.

"Huh," Sid remarks while glaring at the hulking apparition. "That's different."

Sid springs into action. He snatches F4pl0rd's phone, shoves Jamie aside, then bashes through the door with his shoulder. The flimsy wooden thing comes off its hinges and he actually smashes it flat against the opposite wall out in the hallway. He pulls Jamie through the doorway behind him and makes for the stairs as the door tips back to lean at an angle against the jamb it once fit in. They are already to F4pl0rd's apartment door when he hears the hacker shouting after him.

"Hey I need that phone! Pics or didn't happen, man!" F4pl0rd says. "Pics or didn't happen!" Sid stuffs the cell phone into a band attached to his armor's MOLLE webbing and drags Jamie down the stairs faster than anyone other than him ever cares to move. Down two flights, he can hear the transient taunting him without an inkling of urgency.

"Go ahead and run, Sid," the monster says, his feet floating through the wall just above Sid's head. "I know where you're going. I know how this ends. I'll lead you right to me!"

True to his word, the transient does not seem to make much effort to follow as Sid and Jamie run the spiraling gauntlet of ninety degree turns down to the bottom floor and out onto the street in front of the building.

Sid hauls Jamie along toward the utility van, parked at a meter a few blocks away. He finds a city parking attendant writing a ticket next to the van when he gets there. Sid punches the attendant in the face, knocking the man into an unconscious heap in the middle of the street.

"I don't have time for that!" Sid shouts as he tears open the van door and pushes Jamie over the driver's seat to the other side of the van. Once behind the wheel, he fires up the engine and stomps on the gas to get them out of there.

# INT. THE VEIDT INSTITUTE - DAY

"So our choices here are tranny or little kid, right?" Fleabag reasons with difficulty discernable from the way his nostrils flare wolfishly, although he remains mostly human in form. He stands next to the television, hovering menacingly over the good doctor, whom he placed rather firmly on the rec room sofa and ordered not to move. "If I have to have blood on my hands, I pick tranny."

"You're not bumping off one of my patients," Sartorius says. "I won't let it happen."

"You couldn't stop us anyway," Fleabag snorts.

"We're not killing that kid," Helen insists.

"I don't understand all the sudden compassion from you guys," Bruce says. "I mean you're Graveyard. Y'all are shady. You're supposed to do the dirt nobody else can do."

"That was how Walter did things," Helen says.

"Graveyard's been hiding bodies a lot longer than Walter was around."

"How would you know? The Duke had a very different outlook when he was in charge." Helen's cell phone rings. Hurriedly, she answers. "Yeah?" After a pause, she switches to speaker phone. "Sid?"

"Yeah," Sid Hansen says, over what sounds like a hard running engine. "I figured out how we can stop him, or at least slow him down."

"Sid, we know where he came from now. We have—"

"Yeah I know. He's from the future. He told me all about it. Look, I don't have time to chat." An intermission of squealing tires and muffled cursing indicates he is very serious about that claim. "He's reading your reports. That's how he knows where to find us. It was how he found us on the boat, all the places Jamie tried to hide—everywhere."

"What the fuck?" Bruce exclaims, having not quite processed this idea to its logical roots. "You write reports about this shi—yeah I guess you do. That makes sense actually."

"My files?" Helen cringes. "How would he have access to those?"

"He's an agent of Graveyard," Sid says. "From the future."

"Great!" Bruce cheerily exclaims. "So delete that shit and he can never find any of the bloggers and all this just goes away. Problem solved."

But it isn't that simple. It never is. "If he never comes back then none of this ever happens and I never have a reason to delete the files," Helen says.

"I'm sick of this shit! What the fuck is the point of time travel if you can't change shit in the past to make the future different?"

"There's no time for this! Just shut up and listen!" Sid snarls through the phone, clipping the little speaker into fuzzy territory. "Don't delete the files. Just lie in the ones you haven't written yet!"

"What the fuck?" Bruce exclaims, but Helen seems to understand where the kill team is going with this.

"I think I get it. We can't erase what already happened, but we can change what hasn't happened."

"I want you to write a report. Say I lured him into Millennium Park and I found a way to kill him there."

"You got an idea how to kill him?"

"Not the slightest, but if he thinks that's where I stop him, he won't go there. Right?"

# EXT. LAKE SHORE DRIVE - DAY

Sid whips the utility van around a corner onto the freeway, barely clipping a small sedan and sending its panicked driver skidding off the road. Some people don't know anything about combat driving.

"Where are we going?" Jamie screams, looking back at him from the passenger's side rear view mirror, in which the now massive transient emerges, howling like King Kong, from around the corner of a Gold Coast hi-rise in pursuit of the van.

"The park!" Sid growls, wishing the van had a lot more torque and a manual transmission. "I don't think he'll go in there, because that's where he knows I'll kill him!"

"But that's a lie!"

"The truth is a lie! Remember?!"

"What about after that? Just stay in the park forever?!"

"Long enough for Graveyard to bring in some nerve agents so we can spray him down. I still think VX might stop him."

"Chemical weapons?!"

"Fuck yeah, chemical weapons! If I had Tsar Bomba I'd drop that on it too!"

"Maybe I should shoot at it while you drive!"

"That's a terrible idea!"

"Why?"

"Because the back of the van is full of gasoline!" It is. All twenty gas canisters Bruce filled for their plan to burn the codification mainframe were left in the van when Graveyard came to pick them up in helicopters much earlier. Here they remain. Jamie looks into the back of the van to confirm Sid's claim, as if he is wrong by some strange magic, then turns back to the road ahead and mouths a word of alarm as Sid swerves around a slow moving party bus. "Get off the road, ya fucks!"

"This can't possibly get any worse," Jamie cries.

Practically on cue, a Chicago Police cruiser turns onto the freeway right behind them, its sirens singing, lights flashing red and blue.

"It's the police! What do we do now?"

The question sounds like one plus dolphin equals butter knife to Sid's ears. They have a flying harbinger of death spewing black flame right on their ass and Jamie wants to know about the police? The police are fucking rodents. Sid could fight the entire CPD by himself. That's a non-problem right now.

In a blink, the transient is stationed on the dotted line ahead of the van. Sid yanks the steering wheel to avoid the monster as it lashes out with a taloned hand that slides through the passenger's side of the vehicle. Sid reaches to his right and pulls Jamie viciously over to the driver's seat to dodge the raking claws. Pushing the blogger back into place, he glances to the rear of the van and sees that the creature's claws raked four gashes in the paneling near the back doors. It can cut through steel now. That is disconcerting.

# INT. THE VEIDT INSTITUTE - DAY

Dave the analyst plops Helen's laptop case down on the dining table in the rec room. Helen called out to the chopper and had him haul it in. She immediately goes to work unzipping the bag and unfolding the computer from inside.

"What's your Wi-Fi password?" Helen demands. Bruce has to smack Sartorius in the arm to make it clear she's talking to him.

"Uh-uh-oh," the doctor shakes into alert from his daze of irrelevance. "It's hamburgers."

"Hamburgers?" Bruce sneers. "That shit ain't secure."

"It doesn't need to be!" Sartorius says. "We have families in here!"

"Okay, I'm in," Helen calls out, ignoring the bickering. "What should I say?"

"What he said to say. Sid went to Millennium Park. The transient followed him in there and Sid blew him up."

"Blew him up?" Helen asks, already typing headers onto her report.

"I don't know! Sid doesn't know how to kill him!"

"Just say that Kill Team One destroyed the transient by unknown means," Fleabag suggests. "You don't have to know how he did it. Maybe he never told you. It's not like you guys are best friends or anything."

INSERT:
>In the afternoon, Kill Team
>One encountered the unknown
>aggressor again in the
>Millennium Park area of
>downtown Chicago.

"That sounds like shit!" Bruce says, watching over Helen's shoulder as she types.

"I'm not Elmore Leonard, you fuck!" she shouts back. "I don't do fiction!"

"Say they ran into him somewhere else and got chased to the park. It sounded like he was in a car."

INSERT:
>On the following afternoon,
>while accompanying subject
>Chan, Kill Team One
>encountered the unknown
>aggressor at a location near
>downtown Chicago and
>attempted to evade. The
>unknown aggressor pursued
>Kill Team One into Millenium
>Park, where the kill team was
>able to kill the creature by
>unknown means. Kill Team One
>fled the scene and avoided
>capture. We were unable to
>discern his method of
>engagement he employed to
>effectively destroy the
>creature. Subject Chan
>returned to

# #JUSTICE

"I need a pronoun!" Helen says. "What pronoun do I use?"

"This is a real shitty time for that!"

```
INSERT:
        Subject Chan returned to his
        or her residence after
        debriefing and interrogation
        by myself, operators Overton
        and Dunn, as well as
        Codification Agents Remus,
        Byers, and Woznicki.
```

"That's it?" Bruce says. "That's all you got to say?"

"What else would I say?"

"I don't know, but we got to make it believable."

"It's believable!" Helen barks back as she clicks the save button.

"I hope you're right."

# EXT. LAKE SHORE DRIVE - DAY

"Hold on!" Sid says, steering the van around the corner of Monroe and Columbus with a force that slams Jamie against the passenger's side door. The tires screech and gasoline cans topple in the rear of the vehicle. One big red jug wobbles into the front of the van, between the seats, then rolls back as Sid slams down the gas pedal and takes the van up a flight of steps, ascending the grassy hill up into the Lurie Garden. The van bounces furiously up the steps, narrowly fitting between the cement safety wall beside the stairs and the railing that divides the stairway into two sections.

The van hops from the concrete at the top of the steps and smacks down on the brick paved roadway leading deeper into the garden. A sandwich sign relaying lots of useful information about the Monarch Butterfly is obliterated under the van's front bumper. Jamie screams.

"It's just a sign!" Sid yells, veering right to avoid a sprawling bed of foliage. A few small rogue trees stick up in the path ahead, which was laid out for pedestrians and not speeding vans attempting to avoid death ghosts.

The transient appears again in their way, stationed between two short trees like a burning pyre of black flame in the vague shape of a man. Sid hits the breaks and jerks the wheel viciously. He swings the van around in a j-turn that takes out one of the trees. The transient is lost in the spin somewhere while Sid shifts to reverse. The monster phased through the van somewhere in that spin cycle though. Sid checks to see that Jamie remains intact, then sees the transient framed in the windshield as they reverse away at high speed. The monster shakes an angry fist at him.

"What the hell was that?"

"It was one of these," Sid says as he bashes on the brake and twirls the van around again like a squealing top. As the van stabilizes into a forward direction again, Sid is unable to swerve to avoid a big green and white booth featuring a stylized MP logo. The van dashes the tent to pieces, sending plastic rods and bits of wood and polypropylene sailing into the air. A vinyl tarp sign with a big MP logo slaps into the windshield, filling Sid's entire field of view with the words Millennium Park.

When the banner blows away the next sight is that of a wide open grassy field covered by a trellis of crosshatched steel bows. Across the field is a huge amphitheater of reflective steel curves.

"You're insane!" Jamie screams. "You're going to hit somebody!"

That possibility seems unlikely. It's cold out, and there is no significant foot traffic in the park as far as Sid can see. "There's nobody out here!" Sid says as he veers across the field toward a gap in the concrete barrier that partitions this area off from the next section of the park.

He is quickly proven wrong as he sees dozens of people in a small crowd ahead, surrounding a massive blob of polished mirror steel that resembles a giant bean. He doesn't know what that thing is or why people are looking at it, but it's too late to turn back.

The van snaps through some flimsy galvanized steel portable fences, flinging them out of the way and crunching one entirely. Pedestrians run wildly as Sid mashes down on the horn to warn them out of his way. The skyscrapers of the city skyline are only a block beyond the shiny blob of metal in front of them. It would be best to get back there where there are proper streets, as taking the van through the park did not seem to have the desired effect of ending the transient's pursuit.

"DIE!" barks the screaming monster, his giant burning death's head peeking through the ceiling of the van next to Sid's ear. It's on top of the goddamn van.

"Bail!" Sid lets go of the steering wheel and leaps across the van cabin. He pushes Jamie against the passenger door as he rips at the handle and flings them both out onto the grid of concrete squares outside. Sid rolls onto his back and tucks Jamie against him. The dread suit's smooth kydex plates take the brunt of the beating as they slide along the textured ground. Sid comes to a stop and hops up just in time to witness the van, with the demonic mass of fiery darkness riding atop it, crashing through a row of picnic tables and hopping up a few short steps toward the huge mirror blob. The van, the monster, a hundred gallons of gasoline, thousands of small arms rounds, a case of HE grenades, and about forty pounds of plastic explosive all goes airborne and slaloms into the side of the sculpture. By Sid's estimate, it is a spark which ignites the gasoline, then the gasoline explosion which detonates the Semtex. The blast is immense in any case. Whatever that mirror blob thing was, they'll be finding pieces of it on rooftops for years.

Sid watches the flaming wreckage as he pulls Jamie up from the ground.

"Fuck! It's not working," he says. "He followed us into the park anyway. . ."

"Maybe that killed him!" Jamie squeaks out hopefully. "Maybe that was it! Like the reports said!"

Sid shakes his head doubtfully. "I doubt that will even slow him down." What he just said should be patently absurd given that explosion would have stopped a battle tank, but his assertion is proven by the hulking silent shadow that emerges from the inferno ahead. Sid pushes Jamie back toward the pavilion. "We have to make it until he fizzles out again!"

"Stop running, you quisling abomination!" the transient bellows from behind them. The behemoth monster lashes out with his huge hand, snatching up a screaming bystander by the leg and slinging the woman viciously across the park. The transient is off the mark if he wanted to hit either of them, but the bystander wraps around a lamppost nearby and flops to the lawn below as a sack of lifeless broken bones.

# INT. THE VEIDT INSTITUTE - DAY

"Director," says Dave, breaking a tense silence in the rec room. He's looking up from his cell phone. "I think maybe we should turn on the TV. They're talking about the park in the news."

Helen issues a confounded look at Bruce, and he immediately sets on a quest to find the remote for the parlor television, which Fleabag eventually finds for him in the couch cushions. They have to search through the channels manually, because no one present knows which number corresponds to CNN.

When they finally make it through the vast wasteland of game shows, formula comedies about totally unbelievable families, reality shows about totally unbelievable families, and *Sports Center*, they see a blurry live feed of a smoke plume branded by the red and white CNN logo. The crossbar graphic reads *Explosion at Millennium Park*.

Off-screen commentators describe the event, and explore its possible motivations and ramifications as the fire still burns.

"Vaughn, how many bodies can you count at the scene?" asks an unseen woman.

"Well, Brooke. It's hard to say," the fuzzy voice of the correspondent replies. "I haven't seen any bodies just yet, but there are quite a few people who are seriously injured and they may die, which will of course result in a tremendous Nielsen—national tragedy." He quickly corrects himself. "Sorry, Freudian slip."

The crossbar graphic shifts to say Untold Number Killed in Deadly Explosion at Millennium Park.

"It didn't work," Helen whispers. "He followed them into the park anyway."

"Wow, Vaughn, what a tragedy," the CNN anchor gasps overdramatically. "What we're seeing on the feed here in the studio is just really a tragedy. So much tragedy. For those of you just joining us, there has been an explosion in Millennium Park, Chicago, where Vaughn Bondy is live. Someone has blown up the Cloud Gate monument, and I say someone, but that's assuming this wasn't some sort of accident. Could this have been some kind of accident, Vaughn?"

"I think it's safe to rule that out, Brooke. There are just too many other sensational possibilities. It could have been ISIS or Syrian refugees, right-wing extremists, or just a lone individual with inexplicable motivations we'll have to discuss on-air for weeks and-"

"Vaughn, I'm sorry I have to interrupt, but we have a hard break coming up. When we come back, more coverage of this unspeakable massacre brought to you by Dr. Pepper, the one you crave."

CNN fades to a Dr. Pepper commercial, but Bruce isn't sticking around to watch. He's seen enough. He drops the remote down on the couch next to Doris the train spotter and storms off in the direction of the waiting room. Helen snatches his arm in a failed attempt to drag him back.

"What are you doing?" she demands to know.

"It's got to be done," Bruce says, ripping open the door into the hallway. "It's the only way."

"You don't want to do this, Bruce." Helen follows, yanking the door closed behind them, so they're sealed alone in the security hall.

"Nah, I don't. But you already tried your shot, and it didn't take. He's in the park. Now more people are dead. Sid might be dead. This is the only way we know that can stop him."

"Okay, so never mind the terrible moral ramifications. You're talking about creating a time paradox here! We don't know what will happen! Maybe the universe will end!"

"Maybe. But I don't think it'll go that way. The transient already changed shit when he came back and killed all those internet writers. The universe didn't end then. I'm just changing it back the way it was supposed to be."

"Killing a child makes you every bit as bad as him."

Bruce doesn't have anything to say to that. He can only try to contain his own disgust as he continues through the next set of doors. Helen does not try to stop him.

The waiting room is silent, even though a TV is on in the corner and the operator they left standing there is asking Bruce a question. He doesn't hear anything. He's too focused on what he has to do.

# EXT. JAY PRITZKER PAVILION - DAY

The transient towers menacingly over Sid Hansen, howling at the sky as he raises a burning fist to hammer down on Jamie Chan. Sid draws both machetes from their crossed sheaths and intercepts the monster's raging blow in the scissors of both swords. He stands growling back at the monster's ugly face as he strains to hold up the crushing claw. Sid isn't sure which is the reason; his unshakeable will or his ability to clean and press 600lbs, but the transient relents. He is surprised he could interact with the massive fist at all.

Emboldened by the transient's apparent physicality, Sid leaps after the creature's retreating hand and swipes at its face with a silver smelted machete. The blade contacts the transient's typically ethereal flesh, but doesn't even scratch him. It clacks against his cheek like he's made of rock.

"Is that rock hard skin or are you just happy to see me?" Sid says.

"You're a fool, Sid Hansen!" the transient bellows. "Because of you, billions will die!"

"That's a lofty goal. Maybe I better pick up the pace!" Sid jabs a machete point into the transient's non-extant scrotum and is met with a disappointing clack.

"I understand now!" the transient snarls. The monster pounds down at Sid viciously, narrowly missing as he leaps aside of its fist. "It's the only thing I didn't change yet! The only way I haven't tried! I have to kill you too!"

"You've got no chance, you fucking colon impaction." Sid hacks at the transient's neck, but both blades slip through nothing but empty space. "I'll tear your ghost guts out and flush 'em with the rest of the sewage!"

"You have no idea the depth of the darkness within!" the transient roars. "The horror awaits! Prepare for the void!"

The monster unleashes a screaming hate that is somehow tangible even if it has no describable substance. It is not unlike a dragon breathing fire, but cold and empty, devoid of volume or location. It blows away all time and reality as it washes over Sid like a tsunami collapsing over a tiny hut.

# INT. THE VEIDT INSTITUTE - DAY

Bruce studies the waiting room as discreetly as he can, despite all eyes being pointed at him as the newcomer. The secretary remains at her desk, nervously doing nothing, not even wasting time with a magazine or a game of Minesweeper. Ned, the Graveyard operator who remained to guard the room, leans on the counter next to her looking especially bored. His Scorpion submachine gun rests on the countertop, his hand wrapped loosely around the grip. Harper and his mother are still in the corner of the room, only now Harper is watching the television and his mother is knotted more tightly with the intensity of the situation. She sits in one of the little cloth and wood waiting room chairs, her hands resting on the boy's shoulders.

"You find some spooky shit back there?" Ned asks. He has to repeat himself before Bruce actually registers he is saying anything.

"Uh, no," Bruce says. "Looks like this is all just a big goof. Bad intel." Bruce makes his way through the waiting room with a lying smile that makes him sick. He's used it plenty of times in the past, but this time is different. "Hey, uh. . ." Bruce points awkwardly at Harper's mother. He doesn't remember her name, or if she even said what it was. It really doesn't matter. He just needs to get through the next minute, and he'll never have to see her again.

"Michelle," she finishes for him.

"Right. Michelle, can you head back there? The doctor wanted to talk to you about something." It's a shitty lie—shitty because of the hidden intent, but also shitty because of the foundation. Bruce can't imagine any believable reason why the doctor would ask to see some seemingly uninvolved patient in this bizarre situation. He's relying entirely on his authoritative appeal, given the cadre of gun-toting commandos with him, and his friendly attitude to get this one past the goalie. He doesn't want to do this in front of the kid's mom. He can at least try to maintain that standard of decency. "It's all good. I'll watch the little guy for a minute."

There is a moment in which Bruce is unsure whether she believes him. She obviously has some questions about the veracity of his sketchy claim, and she should, but she gets up from her chair to go. She believes him—at least enough. And why wouldn't she? What's the worst that could happen? It's not like someone will shoot her kid in the back of the head while she's in the other room for a second. . .

Christ. Bruce tries to restrict his internal language. Not the kid. The enemy. The target. This is the kind of shit the CIA trained him to do. Don't think of them as people. Think of them as assets, targets, enemy combatants, hostiles, tangos, hajjis, reds, gooks, zipperheads, krauts, lobsters.

Michelle pats the transient on the head and promises she'll be back in just a minute. Then she creeps off through the doors into the security corridor. It won't take long for her to spot the holes in his terrible story once she gets to the rec room. Bruce hopes Helen has the good sense to restrain her back there. He doesn't want this to be any uglier than it needs to be.

He sits down in the same chair Michelle occupied previously and glances over at Ned, who has grown quiet if not altogether edgy. Bruce sees that the operator's gun is now in his hands, rather than resting on the countertop. He cringes and nods toward the back door.

"You want to head back?" Bruce asks. "No reason you need to stick around."

There is a silent interaction which Bruce only witnesses in part, as Ned's eyes shift away from him to the safety glass slit in the security door, then back to him. He loosens his grip on his weapon and allows it to dangle on the strap. It can only mean Helen is back there where Bruce can't see, directing him through the glass.

"We're gonna head back to the rec room," Ned says to the secretary, who responds with some confused stammering. His glare and gun make it much more of a command than a request though, and the secretary complies.

When they're gone, Bruce is alone in the waiting room with the transient and the television. Son Goku is powering up to throw the spirit bomb that obliterates Kid Buu on the TV screen. Bruce thinks this is going to ruin *Dragonball* for him forever. Then he thinks that was a disgusting and selfish thought, because it's hardly the worst part of what he's doing here.

"Which one's your favorite, mister?" the kid says— the transient says.

"Everybody likes Goku the best, right?"

"I guess. I like Vegeta."

"Why?"

The transient shrugs. "Cause his hair is like this." He puts his hands on his head in a maneuver Bruce doesn't understand even a little bit. It's supposed to be some kind of mimicry of Vegeta's bizarre anime widow's peak, but it comes across as nonsense. Kids do stuff like that. From their stilted viewpoint it means something, but they lack the perspective to understand it isn't the same way other people see what they're doing.

Bruce snickers, then catches himself. Don't laugh at the kid. Shoot the kid.

"Have you seen this one before?" Bruce says, trying to make sure the transient is focused on the TV as he grips the pistol concealed in his coat. "This is a really good one."

The transient returns his view to the TV. Bruce quietly pulls his hefty HK from its holster and points the muzzle at the base of the transient's skull.

He has to squeeze the trigger fast. It's like ripping off a Band-Aid. It's got to go. Then he can close his eyes and be done with it forever. He can get the fuck out of here. He can go somewhere and get drunk, because that's what he wants right now. There's not enough beer in the world to get Bruce as drunk as he wants for as long as he wants. He's going to chug a fucking handle of something from Kentucky until he blacks out, and he wants to stay that way until he doesn't remember any of this. Maybe when he pulls the trigger it will all go away anyway and he won't have to erase it that way. Maybe Helen was right. Maybe the universe will collapse on itself or some shit.

Bruce is so lost in thought that he doesn't notice Harper is staring down the gun barrel for a full five seconds. Even when he does register what his eyes are seeing, he doesn't do anything about it. He just holds the gun there. The fucking safety lever is still up. Who the fuck is he kidding? Harper says nothing to him. He just stares with wide blue eyes, too young to understand what's happening or why.

"I—" Bruce starts to say. He doesn't know how to finish that statement. There isn't a statement to finish. He just stops.

Helen Anderson clears her throat across the room. Bruce didn't even realize she came through the door. She could have been there for ten minutes or an hour. He doesn't know how long he has been sitting here, but too much sweat has soaked the underarms of his shirt for it to be the blink it feels like.

"Bruce?" she inquires.

Bruce says nothing. His gun is still trained on the boy's head, haphazardly, one-handed, resting on his lap, aimed by approximation only. He thumbs the safety lever. The hammer is already decocked for double action. The trigger pull is gritty as a cat clawing sandpaper. He doesn't make it to the end.

"I can't fuckin' do it," he says.

"I know." Helen's matter-of-fact inflection further evidences she has been watching him for a long while. Bruce stuffs the HK back in his jacket as he stands and heads for the door. Harper begins to cry as Bruce punches his way out of the Veidt center. He just wants to leave before he sees the mother again. He can't look that lady in the eyes after this.

A dead opossum, squirming with insects and gaseous bloat, with its dead litter of babies still latched to its dried out teats. A man in a burning desert cherishes his necklace of infant feet far above anything ever felt for the babies they came from. He no longer remembers or cares which of them belonged to his own progeny. A boy splits his cock down the middle with rusty kitchen shears because he thinks it is the best way to fuck two girls at the same time. He bleeds out and dies. The teens chained in his filthy cave last almost a week without water. A million screaming bodies melt in nuclear fire. The hobbling radiation poisoned refugees from the outskirts of the blast are easy prey for the rape gangs. Someone grinds nails against a chalkboard. The nails used to be attached to someone else's hand. Tubgirl. Spacedocking. Lena Dunham. A burn victim, her face a mass of featureless collagen, uses a severed penis to pleasure herself. It is shunted with a broken radio antenna. A boy shoots another boy for his bright red sneakers. Upon closer inspection, he sees that they were only colored that way with permanent marker. He pisses on the shoes. A man throws acid on the face of a little girl. Her skin oozes and bleeds. Dozens of onlookers see. Some of them kick her. Boys feed a puppy to a boa constrictor. Then they set the snake on fire with kerosene and matches. The soldiers keep on raping Nanking. Other soldiers set Tokyo on fire.

# #JUSTICE

The smell of children burning is not like other meat, but it is not so horrible when compared to that of a young mother, left spread open by the Japanese, her split-open vagina stuffed with a whole bundle of sharpened bamboo shoots. Maggots writhe in the dried ichor caked in the dirt. Her daughter was too small for penetration, so the soldiers cut her open wider. This is only the beginning of the depravities of the void. The visions go on without slowing, without gaps, without repeat, with absolutely no respite before driving any conscionable man completely insane—or Sid Hansen to boredom.

# EXT. JAY PRITZKER PAVILION - DAY

"Is that it?" Sid dryly intones. He's unimpressed. Frankly, even a little disappointed. Apparently the transient thought it was showing him something disturbing, terrifying, world shatteringly awful. Not so. Sid has seen a bunch of stuff like that before. He's done half of it himself. "That's all you got?"

The transient reels, emitting black mist from its hollowed out shell and breathing heavily. "How?!" the monster bellows. "How can you be so callous?"

"Dipshit, my old man once summoned up an avatar of Nyarlathotep and made me punch it in the face just because." Sid rolls his eyes. "We're talking about the Crawling Chaos here. He literally breathes cosmos crushing forbidden knowledge. You've got what? Some mangled dead people?"

"You're a psychopath!"

"Duh."

The transient howls mournfully at the sky as the black flame consumes its form. "No! I need more time! We were all wrong! The future refused to change! That can only mean. . ." He explodes into a burst of expanding black flame and then fades from existence, leaving no trace he was ever there—no trace but the field of debris and burning steel behind him, and the fleeing tourists screaming and crying throughout the park.

# INT. THE CATACOMBS - DAY

SUPER: The Future

Harper's death scream is loud enough that it bleeds through the sound-proofing of the sensory deprivation pod. Colonel Green does not hurry to climb the ladder and open the hatch. He is hesitant, bordering on averse. He doesn't really need to see what remains inside. For a moment he stops and considers the option to leave it. They'll never need to use the tank for anything again. He could just leave Harper in there and avoid one more nightmare burned into his psyche.

He looks back at the nurse, searching for approval he doesn't need because of his rank, but because he is human. She is already crying. He looks past her to the monitor Harper was always screaming about. Nothing about it has changed. He didn't think it would. He admonishes himself for even looking at all.

Green breathes a sigh at the top of the ladder and reaches for the hatch. He opens it up to see the mess inside and cringes.

What's one more nightmare? A drop in the bucket.

# EXT. JAY PRITZKER PAVILION - DAY

Beneath the trellis of the Pritzker Pavilion, the kill team sheathes his Murder Machetes as Jamie Chan approaches cautiously.

"Is it dead?" Jamie says.

"I'm pretty sure," Sid says, having seen the theatrics the transient made on its final fade from this reality, although he has only vague notions of what actually did the monster in. "I think his time finally ran out for good." He hears the oncoming commotion of ambulances and fire trucks as he scans through the chaos around him for police. "We don't have much time either. We need to get out of here now."

"What about all these people?"

"I'm a killing machine, not a doctor. We need to go."

It is already too late to avoid the police completely. Two uniformed cops are rushing in from the south with guns drawn. They must have run across this by happenstance. If they had any idea what they were getting into they would have come with a whole SWAT team.

"Police! Hands in the air!" one of them shouts. Sid ignores the request, but Jamie complies. That is probably for the best. With the transient dead Jamie should be safe with the cops, though there is the matter of the destroyed monument and any casualties in the park, for which they are both at least partially responsible. They've caught him out in the open in broad daylight, with no good hard cover nearby. Sid considers whipping an FNX from its holster and blowing both these fools away, but he knows Player will find that distasteful. He puts his hands up to buy time as both cops continue to shout directions over the encroaching sirens. "Keep your hands up! Hands up!"

It's funny, but they're blind to Jamie Chan in some way. It's as though they only see the big guy in the scary ninja armor with all the weapons, and a five foot tall unarmed waif is not any kind of a threat to them. Jamie actually backs away from him hesitantly, then more boldly as it becomes clear that neither of the cops' guns are shifting from their present aim at Sid's chest.

"Get on the ground!" left cop shouts.

"On your knees!" right cop yells. It's like a contest for them. Sid glances around to see if any more cops are here yet. If they come a little closer he can seize one of them as a human shield and proceed to beat them both senseless without killing them, but if they do the smart thing and wait for backup he'll be outnumbered and have no choice but to kill his way through whatever fraction of the police department shows up.

Sid lowers himself to his knees, and left cop steps a little closer. It looks like he's taking the bait and making the stupid move even faster than expected. In another few feet Sid will be able to close the gap. . .

A dark shadow is his first inkling of something wrong. Sid notices it before the police can react. The transient. Grey and crusty, but whole again, the monster is somehow fresher than just before. It screams wildly at the police, waving its hands and exhaling blackened fog. "Die! I'll kill you all!"

The cops do the thing anyone would do. They blast the transient with every last bullet they have, but it never stops coming. In the end they're both screaming with the monster standing in their midst, desperately trying to wrestle with something that isn't really there. The ghostly thing looks back at Sid and smiles, for the first time showing some feeling other than melancholy or rage.

Jamie Chan is dead. Dropped by a hail of bullets meant for a thing that can't be shot. The blogger's body lies in a slack-jawed heap on the ground, wide-eyed and unquestionably gone. At least it was quick.

Sid snarls angrily. He stands up and strides toward the transient. The cops are on the verge of hysterics when he smashes their heads together.

"I saw you die!" Sid screams at the monster. The transient only seems to grow confused in response.

"I remember nothing of the sort," he says. He ponders the situation with a perplexed frown as Sid stabs him in the face with a Murder Machete. It does nothing, not even in some mildly therapeutic way. He gives up after a few angry thrusts. Usually stabbing motherfuckers he hates feels good, but this is just air. He wants to kill somebody now. The urge is looming and undeniable. He'll get the name of some human trash from Player before he does anything else. He doesn't have a preference for anyone in particular. He only knows that no matter what they've done, it will not have been terrible enough to make them deserving of what he will do to them. "That means I must come back. I can't imagine why."

"You were right there!" Sid says.

"Chan is dead. I changed everything. I beat you this time. I saved us all."

"I will find you, and I will kill you."

"We were never enemies, even if you never understood. I have to go back now—back to a better future than the one I left."

The transient fades out like a bad special effect, looking content for once. Sid doesn't understand what just happened, or what that thing thinks it accomplished. He doesn't have time to wait around worrying about it either. He makes his way north, for the cover of the auditorium, and steals some clothes from the first person he encounters. He heads over the Fahey bridge to put distance between himself and the park. He calls Helen from the end of Navy Pier and waits on a bench to see the chopper coming in to pick him up. He's only there for ten minutes when F4pl0rd's phone rings. It's F4pl0rd, calling from a different phone.

"Did you get it?" Sid growls. It's too late to help Jamie, regardless of what the hacker found, but Sid is still hungry for a place and a name if F4pl0rd can provide one. He wants to make someone pay for this.

"Are you guys okay?" F4pl0rd asks. "The news says there was a police chase and an explosion. . ."

"Did you get it?" Sid demands. He doesn't care about the stupid details. He doesn't have time for that. He only has time for blood.

"I got it."

"Where?"

# INT. BLACKHAWK - DAY

On the bench seat inside one of Graveyard's unmarked black UH-60 Blackhawk helicopters, Bruce Freeman is trying to cheer Mary Sue out of her depressed funk.

"We could go to the museum before we leave," he suggests. "You like museums, right?"

Mary Sue shrugs, only somewhat despondently—a good sign. Bruce is really glad they didn't bring Mary Sue into that weird remote viewer clinic. She didn't need to see anything that happened in there in her state, especially the part where he almost executed a kid.

"Can we see Sue?"

"Sue?"

"The T-rex at the museum."

"Absolutely we can see Sue the T-rex!" Bruce says. "How about that? And get some of that pellet ice cream! What do they call that stuff?" He is honestly uncertain which one of them he is trying to cheer up after that debacle. It's not that he likes museums so much, though he does like ice cream. He just thinks he can make himself feel better if he makes somebody else feel better.

Helen Anderson interrupts his obtuse beguiling attempts from across the chopper cabin, where she sits between Fleabag and her analyst sidekick. "Bruce, you understand we can never tell you-know-who about you-know-what."

Despite Helen's description lacking any broad specificity or cleverness, Bruce knows exactly what she's talking about. She means they can't tell Sid what they found at that clinic, particularly about the identity of the transient. While Bruce stayed his hand due to sentiment, Sid is a truly remorseless engine of death and destruction capable of atrocities that would break most men.

"I don't think he would do it," Bruce says, uncertain if he is lying to himself.

"He would do it," Helen counters with a serious stare. She's probably right.

They pick the kill team up at the end of Navy Pier, barely touching down on the pavement behind Aon Grand Ballroom for him to hop up the skid into the helicopter. He tears off his sleek dread mask and dumps it on the floor, not caring to take a seat anywhere.

"Wyatt's in Missouri," he growls. "Take me there."

"I wish it were that simple," Helen answers. She hops up from her seat and holds on to a handle on the ceiling as they lift off.

"Who's Wyatt?" Bruce asks. He doesn't expect an answer.

"The mystery man who built the machine for BuzzWorthy," Sid waves him off, then goes back to growling at Helen. "I have the location. If we go now, we might get there in time to murderize the fucker."

"Sid, we already know all about the Missouri IP address," Helen hollers. "My engineers started dismantling the codification engine almost as soon as you told me about it."

"Then what are we waiting for?"

"We already sent operators out there. It was nothing but a proxy server piggybacking off a public Wi-Fi in a coffee shop. All it did was redirect traffic."

"Redirect it to where?"

Helen glances back at Dave the analyst, who is currently viewing their heated discussion over his laptop screen. "Dave, tell him."

The analyst hesitates in the glare of the angry kill team. He gulps. "Jamie Chan's apartment."

"It's a setup," Sid instantaneously responds.

"I don't think so, Sid," Helen argues. "The codification agents were pretty certain about the list. And what about the transient? You really think he wouldn't know who he was looking for coming from the future?"

"He told me himself he didn't understand what he was doing."

"There were no devices on Chan's network redirecting anywhere else," Dave says. "And Chan's laptop contained encrypted copies of the queries from the codification system in Garfield Park. Even the MAC addresses matched up when we checked them. The process for someone to have planted that evidence and not left any trail would be unusually involved."

"But not impossible?"

"Technically no. Aside from physically operating Chan's laptop, I suppose you could use spyware to remotely operate it, then delete the spyware, make an image of the entire drive on an identical drive, and swap them to prevent us from recovering the deleted spyware files. It might be easier to clone the network controller from the laptop and access Chan's Wi-Fi, but you would need the capability to manufacture a chipset from the ground up."

"You mean like somebody who can build a supercomputer?"

"Yes. You're not wrong," Dave says. "He's not wrong," he repeats for Helen more directly. "The measures are just extreme."

"This sounds like paranoia," Helen says. "It took some of the best computer analysts in the world using software backdoors that officially don't exist and heavily armed strike teams illegally searching multiple locations just to dig up what we have. The FBI would not have been able to do what we did. You really think Wyatt saw that coming ahead of time?"

"He accurately predicted an assassin from the future would come back to kill him and successfully outplayed that assassin."

"Or he was Jamie Chan all along, just like all of the evidence suggests. It's a far more believable explanation."

"I think you're underestimating him. If it was my dad, but like a nerd version of my dad, he would be that far ahead of you."

"Where'd the money come from?" Bruce asks. Following the money is always a good strategy. "For the codification mainframe, I mean."

"Offshore bank accounts," Helen says. "The accounts and pins were all found on Jamie Chan's laptop. Guys, I know you don't want to believe it was Chan, but it was Chan."

"I didn't kill Chan," Sid says. "The recording said only I can kill Wyatt."

"It said only you can *stop* Wyatt. I think this is how you did."

"If Chan was Wyatt and the transient killed Chan, then the transient prevented the nightmare future, so he would have never come back to kill Chan in the first place, which means the nightmare future still happens. So that means he must have nailed the wrong guy."

"If that's true it means it's impossible to prevent the future no matter what we do."

"That zany time paradox again," Bruce says.

"No," Mary Sue says, shifting everyone's attention to her in some surprise. "The future he came from could be just one possible future."

"Hey! There you go!" Bruce says. "That's the spirit. It's some other future. Alternate universe shit. He wasn't just a ghost from the future. He was a ghost from the future from some other dimension too. See? So now it makes sense."

"I hope so," Mary Sue says, looking glassy-eyed at the cabin floor.

# INT. FIREHOUSE - DAY

Sid rises from his bed on the top floor of the firehouse and grabs his towel for a trip down the hall to the shower. Behind him, Sapphire moans in the sheets.

"You were kinda rough last night," she says, barely keeping her eyes open.

"Yeah. Work stress," Sid says.

"What is it that you do?"

"Backend analytics." This is something Bruce told him to say if asked about his job. The answer is apparently something so boring and sophisticated that hardly anyone will ever inquire further about it, eliminating the need for a complex backstory and research. Also, butts. Indeed, Sapphire doesn't want to know anything more after that initial question, so Sid leaves her money on the nightstand beside her and then walks down the hall for a shower.

He's still a little angry from Chicago, despite taking out his frustration on a serial child molester, two gang bangers that killed a grandma in a crossfire, and a heroin dealer. Player located them all for him quite easily, using the satellite. He beat, crushed, twisted and eviscerated them all over the course of the last few nights, then pounded Sapphire through the bed as soon as she was available.

Early TV news reports notwithstanding, there was only one death in Millennium Park. When Graveyard circulated the false story that the accident was caused by a drunk driver, the big news channels almost immediately lost interest. Bruce seemed annoyed by that for some reason Sid does not understand.

Sid discovers Mary Sue already occupying the bathroom down the hall, only she hardly looks like Mary Sue at all. She's wearing even teenier shorts than usual, with black suspenders and a teensy yellow vest that barely contains her epic breasts. Her legs are covered by heavy white boots and nude-colored thigh high stockings. She is wearing a purple wig. She looks ridiculous. Sexy, but ridiculous.

"What the hell is this?" Sid questions. He wants to know about the hokey outfit and also why she's in his bathroom instead of the one downstairs, but he'll settle for either explanation.

"Bruce made the downstairs bathroom, um," she purses her lips while questing for the word. "Malodorous." This is doubtlessly related to the double stacked boxes of carry-out extra-extra-wet *retarded hot* chicken wings Sid noticed in the downstairs refrigerator late last night. Sid tried one and didn't get what all the fuss is about, but at least the bathroom mystery is solved.

"And the get-up?" he asks, moving on to the next detail.

"This is my Faye Valentine cosplay. I'm going to an anime convention." That's a good thing, Sid thinks. Mary Sue was unusually quiet for the last few days, which she spent watching ignorant Japanese cartoons surrounded by scented candles and holding a stuffed bear. Now she seems back to her regular perky self.

"I see. . ." Sid says, eye humping her from the boots to the absurd purple wig. She shuts the bathroom door in his face. He sighs, ties his towel tighter, and heads downstairs to fry up some bacon.

Bruce is lying across the couch on the first floor. Something called *Law and Order: Stenography Department* is muted on the big TV in front of him. Sid lights up a burner and goes digging through the fridge.

"Homie," Bruce groans out a warning. "Whatever you do, don't eat the retarded wings. They make you pay."

"I told you it was a mistake," the Player says from the conference phone on Mary Sue's unoccupied desk.

"They burn going in and they burn coming out. Should 'a called them things *full* retard wings."

"Sid, I've got something I want you to look into," Player says. "I'm tracking a New York art dealer rumored to be running a Ponzi scheme under a fake name."

"What's a ponzi scheme?" Sid says, unwrapping a package of bacon on the countertop near the stove.

"Nobody fuckin' knows," Bruce says.

"It's an investment con in which the con artist pays older investors with money from new investors," Player explains in total disregard for Bruce's assertion.

"Sounds boring," Sid says.

"White collar crime is serious, Sid. Thousands of people could lose everything in this scam."

"Whatever. I'll kill him. Where's he live?"

"I don't want you to kill him. We don't even know if he's guilty yet. I need you to approach him about an investment so we can try to track where the money goes."

"I don't do investments. You got anything else? Is there an experimental warframe I can blow up, or a factory that kidnaps little orphan girls and mutates them into synthowombs for genobeasts?"

"What the fuck?" Bruce yelps. "That can't be a real thing."

"Not anymore it's not."

"I think he's making that one up too," Player agrees.

"I can never tell," Bruce says.

"What are you doing today?" Sid asks of Bruce, attempting to steer the conversation away from things he doesn't want to do.

"I'm going out to get some Sanwa parts. I busted my fightstick last night."

"That sounds painful."

The Player is not ignored so easily. "Sid, you can't just pick the missions you think sound interesting."

"Watch me."

"Watch me cut off the whore money."

"Because that went so well this time."

"You saved the world!"

"By failing to stop another guy from saving it. I could have stayed here and nailed Sapphire all week, and the transient would have killed Chan-Wyatt-whoever, and we would be exactly where we are now—except I wouldn't have blown that dumb statue up."

"He's got you there," Bruce says. "We didn't accomplish shit in Chicago."

"So you're sure now that Chan was really Wyatt? " Player says. "I thought you didn't believe that."

"The eggheads at Graveyard say so. Mary Sue says it makes sense. They understand it all better than I do. Something-something time travel something-something multiple universes. Wyatt's dead. Toilet future averted. We can all go back to what we do best."

"I'm not giving you a dime for prostitutes until you look into this Ponzi scheme."

"Fine," Sid relents as he places strips of bacon into a crackling frying pan. "There has to be a better way for me to get laid."

"Until you find one, you do what I say."

"You could join one of those pickup artist groups," Bruce suggests.

"Do *not* join one of those groups," Player says.

"I think I need to hear more about this. . ." Sid says.

# EXT. LEVEL UP GAMES - DAY

"So this place is better than GameStop?" Sid asks, heading through the parking lot toward the small boutique shop with its box-light sign. The letter **P** looks like a video game directional pad.

"Yeah, man," Bruce says. "GameStop is for noobs. I thought you knew that."

Sid shakes his head as they enter the store, which looks and smells just like a GameStop store. It has that same hint of body odor and warm electronics. The shelves and peg hooks are packed with troves of colorful video game paraphernalia all around him. The selection of actual video games is noticeably lacking, with over half of the space dedicated to sculptures, bobble heads, t-shirts and other tie-in merchandise.

The clerk behind the counter even greets them with the standard GameStop sales pitch, delivered in the trademarked hopeless demeanor of all GameStop employees. "Welcome to Level Up, where you can preorder *No Man's Sky 2*. It's actually a game this time."

"Quit fucking with me, Dennis," Bruce says. "Nobody wants that shit."

"Nobody wants your shit," the clerk answers, surprisingly out of form for a retail clerk. Dennis? Sid remembers that name. Dennis was the name of the GameStop district manager who got Bruce and Sid jobs at the company in the first place—Bruce's brother-in-law.

"You're the same Dennis?" Sid says, eyeballing the portly man. Dennis is a haphazardly shaven man, with a mixed complexion and thick hipster glasses. He certainly looks like he could be related to Bruce. "GameStop Dennis?"

"Fuck that company, man," Dennis says. "I'm on my own now. One hundred percent small business, mom and pop, ground floor, run by players for the players. This is it."

"That's my boy, right there," Bruce says.

"You seen this shit, man?" Dennis says, pointing behind him to a flat panel monitor mounted above the store's main counter. On the screen is a high resolution image of an animated person fiddling with what appears to be a video game console in a digitized living room setting. A real-life, albeit low-resolution, talking head occupies the corner of the picture, conversing heatedly with another party who cannot be seen.

"It has the red ring of death. What do I do?" the talking head says. "I think the warranty is expired."

"The fuck is this?" Bruce asks.

"This is *Video Game: The Video Game*," Dennis answers. "This guy has been streaming it all weekend. The point of the game is you play video games. Shit's blowing up the indie scene."

"Doesn't look like he's playing shit."

"Yeah, the console broke and Microsoft don't want to fix it."

"The video game in the video game is broken?"

"Yeah. That's part of the game. Your system breaks sometimes, and you got to get that shit fixed."

"Man, that's fucked up. You got my fightstick parts?"

"Yeah. Got that shit in the back. You hear about Shankeesha?" Dennis says as he saunters toward the back of the store.

"No. What?" Bruce asks, seemingly taken off guard.

"She got engaged."

"No shit? To the white boy with the—what is it? The peg leg company?" Sid has no interest in this gossip. He wanders away from the counter a few feet, until his eyes catch on two pretty girls walking past the store's front window. He slowly heads for the front door to get a better look.

"Prosthetics. That shit ain't no joke. He makin' paper. You got to see this ring he got her. You talkin' about ice—homeboy got her a skating rink." Sid determines the girls, roughly his age, are headed to the nail salon a few stores down the strip mall. He considers following them. Nothing in Level Up interests him. "It's a blood diamond too."

Suddenly, something in Level Up *does* interest Sid. It interests him very much. The comment passed Bruce's attention without throwing up any flags, but Bruce doesn't remember things like Sid.

"A blood diamond?" Sid says. "Why a blood diamond?"

Dennis shrugs. "Bitches like shiny shit."

"Heard that," Bruce laments.

"They want blood diamonds more than other diamonds?" Sid presses.

"Yeah, man. It's the only kind that's worth anything. I mean, somebody died for it."

"Where did you hear that?" Sid narrows his eyes at Dennis, turning the tone of the conversation toward darker territory.

"I don't know. It's just what everybody says."

"You alright?" Bruce asks. "What's the deal?"

It could be nothing. It could be that Sid is just being paranoid. It could be that Chan successfully implemented this little change before everything that happened this week—or it could be something.

"It's nothing," Sid says, reassuring Bruce and Dennis. The others quickly return to their idle chitchat, but Sid can't help the feeling that Wyatt is still out there somewhere.

NEXT:

Bad Harem

Made in the USA
Monee, IL
04 September 2021